To Catch A Spy
and Traitor

TO CATCH A SPY AND TRAITOR

by

Toby Oliver

Published in 2020

ISBN: 9798682513734 (paperback)

If you live amongst wolves, you
have to act like a wolf.
Nikita Khrushchev

For us in Russia, communism is a dead dog, while,
for many people in the West, it is still a living lion.
Aleksandr Solzhenitsyn

With grateful thanks to David, Jill, Heather
and Carol for all their support

AUTHOR'S NOTE

Although this is a work of fiction, I have tried to represent the historical background as it actually was. For this purpose, I have relied on books that were based on first-hand experience and provided documentary evidence.

CHAPTER 1

Mount Street, Mayfair, West London
July 1962

The morning had started off like many others with a routine call from an MI5 colleague, Bradley Duncan, suggesting they met up for breakfast at his flat. As planned, Joyce arrived precisely at 8.00 am. She pressed the doorbell a couple of times, but when he failed to answer, she decided to let herself in using a spare key.

'Brad, are you there? Are you okay?' she called out.

Met by a wall of silence, she slipped a Walther PPK from her handbag and began carefully edging her way along the hallway.

'Brad,' she repeated. 'Where the hell are you?'

Joyce waited for a second, but there was still no response. So, she continued quietly through the flat toward the kitchen, which was normally a warm cosy hub. Bradley was an accomplished chef. On the table, there was a loaf of freshly baked bread and eggs waiting to be cooked for their breakfast, but still no sign of Bradley.

She turned and made her way to the living room. Joyce paused in the hallway and peered through the crack of the door. She called his name again before tentatively nudging the door wide open.

Bradley's body was slumped awkwardly against the dining table, with blood stains splattered across the carpet and up the walls. Joyce caught her breath at the chilling scene and took a moment, trying to take it all in.

Fully expecting her to join him for breakfast, she could only imagine perhaps he'd let his guard down and unwittingly opened the door to his assassin.

His killer had slugged two bullets into him the first, placed with deadly precision just above the bridge of his nose, the other had slammed into his chest. It certainly had all the hallmarks of a professional hit. Bradley hadn't stood a chance. Whoever it was, certainly wouldn't have risked hanging around too long after taking him out.

Blood had soaked his shirt, leaving only sparse patches of white cotton through the staining. The mop of dark hair, the once striking hazel eyes, and aquiline features had not only belied his thirty-nine years, but made him extremely popular with the opposite sex.

Steeling herself, Joyce took a sharp intake of breath before checking for a pulse. She didn't quite know why, but somehow, it seemed the right thing to do. His flesh was still warm; her fingers recoiled instinctively.

He'd called her earlier to suggest meeting up for breakfast to discuss, "their mutual friend".

Their so-called "mutual" friend was a euphemism for Alexei Ivanov, a high-ranking KGB officer based at the Soviet Embassy. He was viewed as a prized asset, a double agent who was now working for British Intelligence.

Although Bradley had seemed a little guarded, Joyce had simply put it down to the fact they were talking on an open line. There'd been nothing to indicate he was uneasy, or that his life was in imminent danger. If there had, Bradley wouldn't have wasted his time calling her at home but raised the alarm directly with MI5's HQ.

In the past, there had been the odd occasion when Joyce had feared Bradley might well be playing above his operational experience and capability. That said, despite the occasional misgivings, he really hadn't put a foot wrong handling Ivanov. A tricky task at the best of times, even for more seasoned officers.

Joyce had never considered him to be quite up to the general rough house of field intelligence. Although, to his credit, even under increasing pressure to deliver results running their volatile Russian, Bradley had never once let down either the Service or Ivanov.

The majority of his most insightful reports were the result of spending many a booze-filled evening in the company of Comrade Ivanov, exchanging endless shots of vodka and whisky. Joyce still wasn't quite sure how Bradley had managed to keep a clear head during their alcohol-filled late-night sessions, but somehow, he had.

As the Russian's tongue loosened, Bradley's reports had frequently contained the odd gem, including a long-held suspicion the relationship between the KGB and its diplomatic staff at the London Embassy was even more dysfunctional and corrosive than those between MI5 and its overseas sister organisation MI6.

Taking a step back from her ex-colleague's body, she steeled herself. There was still a job to be done. Her attention turned to the dining table. There were two place settings in readiness for their breakfast. She lightly brushed her fingers over the sleek silver teapot; it was still piping hot.

Her grasp tightened around the PPK as she made her way back out into the hallway. She swiftly checked out the remaining rooms, ending up in the small study cum library.

Walking over to the desk, she picked up the phone and unscrewed both the receiver and earpiece. Having satisfied herself the line hadn't been bugged, Joyce bypassed MI5's switchboard and dialled the Director General Sir Spencer Hall's personal number.

Even within British Intelligence circles, direct access to the DG was on a strictly limited basis.

Dawn Abrams, Spencer's secretary, took the call. 'DG's office.'

'Blackdown is dead, repeat *dead*,' Joyce announced, her voice devoid of emotion.

Blackdown was Bradley's codename.

There was a moment's hesitation. 'Where?' Dawn queried.

'His flat.'

'Are *you* in danger?'

'No.'

'Are you able to sit tight?'

'For the time being.'

'Leave it with me,' Dawn said, abruptly ending the call.

With an MI5 officer down, it was standard procedure to inform Scotland Yard's Special Branch. They were effectively the police arm of the security services. It wasn't so much a courtesy call, but more a means of ensuring the murder scene would be tidied up with a minimum of fuss. To keep things tight, without having to involve the local police.

Joyce held the receiver a while before slowly replacing it on the cradle. Time wasn't on her side. She only had a small window of opportunity to lift anything from the flat, and, in particular, stuff Spencer might wish to keep strictly in-house, before Special Branch arrived to seal the flat.

Bradley's death had ratcheted up the stakes;

within a few days, all hell would break loose. For Bradley wasn't just a member of British Intelligence killed in the line of duty, he was also a close friend of the Prime Minister, Gerry Hawley. News of his murder would set the Whitehall machine in motion, if not panic.

His death wasn't only brutal, but for once, understandably, the press would have a complete field day.

On a professional level, Joyce had initially viewed using Bradley as something of a high-risk strategy. It wasn't just his closeness to the PM; he was also a leading light on London's social scene.

At face value, he was probably one of the very last people on earth anyone would have been considered to be potential MI5 material.

The decision to approach Bradley had been the Director General's and his alone. His subsequent involvement with the Security Service had been a tightknit secret, even within British Intelligence circles, known only to a select few. A secret so sensitive that Joyce suspected even the Prime Minister might not be aware of his friend's double life.

Whatever the rights or wrongs surrounding his recruitment to the Service, and her initial doubts about his suitability, he'd proved her wrong, time and again, eventually winning her over by his sheer exuberance and commitment.

In private, Bradley had been great company and a great if not hilarious raconteur. Famous names had dropped from his lips like autumn leaves as he recounted some scandalous anecdote. However, he knew where to draw the line, and since his recruitment to MI5, he had remained utterly discreet regarding his close friendship with the Prime Minister, which had been totally sacrosanct.

Bradley had approached everything British Intelligence had ultimately thrown at him not only with a profound loyalty, but also integrity. Which sadly, wasn't always necessarily the case with the old and bold, more experienced members of the Service.

Bradley had paid the ultimate price; his tragic loss reverberated deeply with her.

CHAPTER 2

South Kensington, South West London

On his way to the Soviet Embassy, Alexei Ivanov paused to light a cigarette in a quiet residential street, a short distance from Kensington High Street. He took a moment making sure it was safe, before slipping into a phone box.

Ivanov wasn't overly tall, but sturdy in build and broad-shouldered with a serious, almost permanently, melancholy expression. Closing the door behind him, Ivanov paused, took a deep breath, swallowed uneasily, and reached into his trouser pockets for some loose change. His pulse was racing, and he could feel the sweat on the back of his neck. Picking up the receiver, he waited for the tone before dialling Westminster 1275. It was Bradley Duncan's contact number, his MI5 handler.

Waiting impatiently for a response, Ivanov

peered anxiously through the small square phone box windows, in the hope he'd managed to give his KGB tail the slip.

It seemed like an eternity but in reality was probably no more than a few seconds before a stranger's voice, the duty officer, Jed Carter answered his call.

Ivanov's hand shook as he clumsily inserted the loose change into the coin slot. 'Where's Blackdown?' he blurted out.

'I'm afraid he's not available right now. How can I help you?'

A beat of silence fell between them before Ivanov broke it. 'I need a meeting!' he said bluntly.

'When?'

'Today! It has to be *today*!'

'Are you able to hold on?'

'Yes…yes.'

Hearing a rapid series of clicks on the line, Ivanov closed his eyes in exasperation. A lot was riding on their response. He might not get another opportunity to get things moving.

Eventually, a vaguely familiar voice punctured the interminable clicks and crackles. 'I understand you have a problem.'

'Well, you could say that, *yes*!' he said irritably.

'I understand you need to meet us urgently?'

Ivanov grunted his response.

'Do you know the York Hotel in Kington Square?'

'I do.'

'Good. Then I'll see you there.'

'When?'

'Oh, shall we say lunchtime, about 12.45?' came the considered reply.

Ivanov shot back the cuff of his shirt and checked his watch. 'If I run into trouble, I might not make it on time.'

'Then we'll wait for you.'

'And how will I recognise you?'

'My dear Alexei, I'd be *very* surprised if not a little disappointed if you didn't recognise me!'

Suddenly, the owner of the calm, velvety timbre fell into place; it belonged to Sir Spencer Hall, the Director General of MI5. He was already just about clinging on by his fingertips, but now this only served to heighten his anxiety. Spencer, rarely, if ever, personally met or *officially* spoke to his agents about business. It just wasn't done.

As if slightly alarmed by the protracted silence on the line, Spencer pressed, 'Alexei, are you still there?'

It was just enough to jolt Ivanov out of his reverie. 'I'm…I'm sorry,' he stammered distractedly. 'Yes, I am.'

'You do recognise *me*, don't *you?*' Spencer repeated.

'How could I forget,' the Russian snorted uneasily.

'Then I take it, we're agreed then…12.45 at the York Hotel?

'Yes.'

'I'll be in the foyer. When you see me, just walk straight through to the rear exit onto Mercer Street. Is that clear?'

'And then what?'

'We'll take it from there.'

'And what happens if I can't shake off my surveillance?'

'Well, I suppose as long as your Russian friends don't decide to kill you, I suggest you continue following normal procedure and contact us in the usual way.'

There were so many questions buzzing away inside Ivanov's head. Whatever way he looked at it, he was in deep, deep trouble. Spencer's deadpan delivery wasn't exactly helping.

'What if there's a change of plan your end?' Ivanov persisted, catching sight of an elderly woman waiting outside to use the phone box.

'Just as long as you're able to give *your* people the slip, then I guarantee there won't be a change of plan,' Spencer said, ending the call.

Ivanov replaced the receiver, turned, and held the heavy metal door open for the woman. She thanked him.

He stood for a moment, recalling all too clearly his somewhat brief encounter with Britain's spymaster at a diplomatic reception hosted by the Foreign Office in Whitehall. As these things tended to be, it had been quite a grand affair. The Director

General's identity was a closely guarded secret, and he rarely, if ever, ventured into the limelight. As a rule, Spencer worked quietly, away from public attention, and only a select few were familiar with the name of MI5's all-powerful Director General. To the majority of guests, he had simply been just another indistinguishable civil servant or perhaps some low-ranking diplomat.

Spencer had arrived at the reception in the company of a tall, attractive woman, whom Ivanov had later discovered was an ex-CIA agent by the name of Virginia Dudley. The latest KGB reports confirmed they had been in an on-and-off relationship for several years, but there were also ongoing doubts about the seriousness of their affair. He valued his independence and, in the main, lead a relatively solitary life by choice. Whatever the real truth of the matter, they had seemed comfortable in each other's company.

Spencer had delivered everything Ivanov expected – a touch of mystery, charm, and a certain introspection. The smile was half pleasant, half croc-odile. On the surface, he'd appeared entirely affa-ble, even engaging, but it was evident that he was a man accustomed to commanding an audience, and respect.

Watching Spencer work his way back through the crowded reception, Demetri Smolin, the KGB's resident-designate at the London Station and *supposed* Cultural Secretary, had explained to Ivanov that you never quite knew what you were going to get with Spencer. The smooth, urbane character, who seemed totally at ease with the great and good on the diplomatic circuit, or the tough, ruthless spymaster, who wouldn't hesitate to destroy anyone who crossed his path. Spencer's famous charisma, Smolin had told the younger man, was only deployed as and when required. Behind the slick, eloquent exterior was an ironclad street fighter, albeit one who now happened to wear an expensive Savile Row suit.

CHAPTER 3

The Soviet Embassy
Kensington, South West London

The Soviet Embassy was located in an exclusive, tree-lined avenue half a mile long, in the so-called heart of Embassy land, owned by the Crown Estate, at No.13 Kensington Palace Gardens. The Consulate was conveniently situated nearby at No.5.

A little before midday, Ivanov made his way out of his office and down toward the main gate. For all intents and purposes, it seemed much like any other day. On seeing him, the uniformed guard sprang rigidly to attention.

As usual, Ivanov stopped to pass the time of day with the young man. In fact, he had always made a point of doing so. In many ways, it was perhaps a small but at the same time significant gesture from a high-ranking KGB officer. Many of his colleagues rarely, if ever, gave their in-house security guards the time of day.

As a consequence, his apparent keen interest in their welfare had made him genuinely popular with the Embassy's military guards. He regularly made enquiries about their duties and, more astutely, never failed to make a point of asking about their families, many of whom had remained many thousands of miles away back home in Russia. It was a smooth touch, but one which had ultimately made a lasting impression on the young men. Ivanov's interest was, in part, entirely genuine, but it also made them far less inclined to take an active interest in his regular comings and goings.

However, his overriding motive was explicitly aimed at MI5 and Scotland Yard's so-called "watchers team" round-the-clock surveillance of the Embassy, positioned in a building owned by Her Majesty's government. The activities of both the Embassy and Consulate staff were meticulously monitored and recorded through telescopic lenses.

Apart from the twenty-four-hour surveillance, specialist Post Office engineers embedded within the Security Service had successfully tapped into their respective telegraph and telephone communications. Given the ongoing tensions of the Cold War, bugging on an industrial scale came with the territory and was no more than either side expected. The US and British embassies in Moscow were also under the same close scrutiny.

Ivanov viewed their ongoing presence as a reassuring lifeline, that help was never too far away.

He stayed chatting to the guard just long enough to satisfy himself; his British friends would have picked up on him before leaving the compound and heading toward Kensington High Street.

Shortly after crossing the road, it swiftly became apparent he was under surveillance of a slightly different kind—that of his KGB colleagues. Over the last forty-eight hours, the drill and routine were precisely the same. But it was always a new face on the scene, and, more crucially, someone out-with the Embassy's residential KGB staff. All of whom he knew personally.

There was only one logical conclusion. He had been in the game long enough to know that a specially selected team had been drafted in from Moscow Central. However, what wasn't quite so clear to him was, why they were playing such an obvious game of wanting to be seen? So far, they had made little, if any, effort to disguise their presence or intentions.

Just quite what his British "watchers" were making of their overt and—on the surface at least—somewhat bodged surveillance tactics was open to conjecture. To the untrained eye, the average passer-by wouldn't have given his tail so much as a second glance. However, today's new face stuck out a mile. Ivanov picked up on him immediately. The way he dressed, the way he moved, and—especially to a Russian—his Turkic features made him stand out from the crowd.

Ivanov gave no sign of noticing he'd picked up on him and continued walking. The only thing that was seriously playing on his mind was why he hadn't managed to pick up on his MI5 security shadow. *Where the hell were they?*

On reaching the High Street, Ivanov paused at the kerb for the traffic lights to change. He needed to focus, to keep a grip, and swiftly slipped off his wristwatch. Clasping it tightly in his left hand, he figured it'd make it a little less visible that he needed to keep a constant check on the time.

When the traffic lights changed to red, Ivanov darted across the road and began weaving his way along the crowded High Street. Now and then, he stopped occasionally to check out a shop window display. His KGB tail continued to retain a discreet distance between him. It was no more than a game of cat and mouse.

Ivanov decided he needed to mix things up a little and stopped to light a cigarette, as his KGB tail made to a nearby news stand to buy a paper. He quietly smiled to himself, exhaling a stream of smoke. Taking another slow draw on his freshly lit cigarette, he retraced his steps back down the High Street, past his shadow, before heading into Gameton's, a vast, quirky, old-fashioned emporium selling an eclectic mix of antiques.

It had become one of his favourite haunts. At

least it was on a Saturday afternoon, if Chelsea was not playing a home match at Stamford Bridge, which he considered to be nothing less than sacred.

Football aside, since their arrival in London almost a year ago now, Ivanov and his wife, Tasha, had ended up spending a small fortune at the emporium; it was usually stuff Tasha intended on shipping back to Moscow. In his opinion, she had a somewhat scattergun approach to buying. By instinct, he wasn't an impulsive buyer, preferring to select a few items he thought to be particularly special.

However, like many of their Embassy friends and colleagues, on a somewhat superficial level, they continued to adhere to Moscow's hard-line communist doctrine against the so-called evils of capitalist consumerism. But, once away from the constraints of "Mother Russia", free from the continual shortages and restrictions at home, they didn't hesitate in making a beeline for all the West had to offer and stocked up on just about everything missing from their daily lives.

Back home in Moscow, the vast GUM store on Red Square—with its precious, albeit limited supply of luxury goods—frequently resulted in queues extending across the vast Square. Russian officials and Western diplomats alike jokingly nicknamed the GUM's so-called prized pungent aftershave as "Stalin's breath".

In the past, the life of a quasi-diplomat in the

West had many benefits, including keeping his wife and family happy. London, as had his previous appointment in Paris, was charged with a sense of unbridled freedom.

After initially holding back a little, his KGB colleague joined him inside the Emporium. Ivanov was chatting animatedly to an attractive shop assistant, apparently discussing the merits of a Victorian oil painting framed in an ornate gilt frame.

'Maybe if the price were right, I'd consider buying it.' Ivanov smiled at her with a shrug.

She echoed his smile, assuring him that as a valued Gameton's customer,

there was always a deal to be made.

'Yes, I'm sure there is.' He thanked her and promised to return with his wife next week.

Stepping back outside the Emporium, Ivanov glanced back through the glass doors, briefly making eye contact with his Soviet tail. There was a slight, lame flicker of recognition between them.

Ivanov discarded his spent cigarette and crushed his under his foot, hesitating a moment considering his options. If he couldn't shift the bastard, then he'd have to abort his meeting with Spencer Hall. *And then what? God only knew!*

The KGB was playing mind games with him—of that, he was sure—before moving in for the kill.

Ivanov found himself toying with the idea of boarding a bus but decided against it. Instead, he started heading back along the High Street toward the massive, imposing art deco façade of Barker's department store, where he knew taxis would be two a penny plying for trade.

Nearing the main entrance, he spotted an approaching taxi emitting a yellow light, meaning it was for hire. Ivanov raised his hand. The cabbie swung out of the line of traffic and drew in alongside him at the kerb.

'Where to, Guv?'

'The Imperial War Museum, Kennington.'

'Okay, mate, hop in,' he said, switching off the "for hire" light.

CHAPTER 4

York Hotel
Kington Square, South West London

With Ivanov running late for their meeting, Spencer decided he might as well order more coffee. It wasn't particularly pleasant, but then again, he figured it probably wouldn't hurt to have another caffeine fix.

Having already steadily worked his way through a batch of this morning's newspapers, as a last resort, he began tackling the *Daily Telegraph*'s baffling cryptic crossword.

Spencer had never particularly enjoyed doing them and, like now, would typically have had to have been bored out of his skull before attempting to do one. He had always viewed them as being akin to mental combat between both the puzzle setter and the solver.

Thoughtfully slipping the top of his pen lightly between his lips, he carefully started wracking his brain over the first clue. During the War, the cryptic puzzles had proved especially popular with the various egghead codebreakers at the ultra-secret Bletchley Park. The rural estate had been purchased by the government back in 1938. The charming nineteenth-century mansion and numerous outbuildings had housed Britain's Code and Cypher School, or BC&CS, as it was more commonly known in government circles. Their work in penetrating the secret communications of the Axis powers had, in effect, shortened the war by at least two to four years.

Perhaps unsurprisingly, Spencer had never entirely shared their enthusiasm or, he readily admitted, their intellect to breeze through the puzzles with such apparent consummate ease.

The waitress returned across the foyer with his freshly brewed coffee. He thanked her and paid up his bill with a handsome tip. As he folded his black leather wallet, a sudden movement caught his eye as a tall, elegant blonde swept through the revolving doors into the foyer. Spencer glanced across at her; their eyes met briefly in recognition. She was tall and slender, with sharp, enviously angular bone structure.

Joyce Leader wasn't only one of his inner circle; he had also entrusted her with overseeing Bradley's day-to-day handling of Ivanov.

She was dressed immaculately in an expensive figure-hugging Givenchy suit. He smiled to himself. It was the kind of couture outfit she could never have afforded on a basic Civil Servant's salary, nor on the rather meagre additional MI5 dress code allowance. Comments had been made in the past. Spencer had always brushed them aside, as he was all too aware Joyce had a private income. In fact, a *very* substantial one. The origin of her inherited fortune probably wouldn't stand up to too much scrutiny, but that was entirely on a need-to-know basis.

Over the years, her beauty had matured but remained somehow undiminished. Joyce still looked incredible, and without exception, every male and female head turned in her wake as she sauntered slowly across the plush carpeted foyer toward him.

'Darling, how lovely to see you again.' Joyce smiled, planting a fleeting, perfunctory kiss on each of his cheeks.

'You're late,' he hissed beneath his breath.

'Yes, I'm sorry,' Joyce apologised, seating herself in the dark green Chesterfield styled leather chair next to his. 'Have you missed me?'

'I was almost beginning to think that you'd stood me up!' His voice was just loud enough for anyone within earshot to catch his words.

'Traffic, darling, it was down to the traffic. I'm so sorry,' she said, placing an expensive black patent handbag beside her matching stilettoed feet.

'Coffee or tea?' he offered.

'No, thanks, I'm fine.'

Lowering his voice again, Spencer rasped, 'What's been going on, *Jo*? Where the *hell* have you been?'

'Waiting for a bloody update on Ivanov, that's what!'

He leaned forward slightly. 'So, where are we? Has he managed to give them the slip?'

Joyce heaved her shoulders. 'Well, you always said he was pretty slick.'

'Slick, maybe, but where *is he*?'

Catching the sudden wary glint in her Delft-blue eyes, Spencer offered up a half-hearted laugh. 'For Christ's sake, Jo, why not just spit it out? You never know, it might not taste so bad.'

'We've lost him,' she said bleakly.

'Where about?'

'You really don't want to know.'

'Try me.'

She thoughtfully sucked in her lower lip. 'Outside Barkers.'

'Are you being serious? It's a stone's throw away from the ruddy Embassy!' Her silence was answer enough. 'And what about the KGB?'

'He's given both of us the slip.'

'Are you sure?'

'Yes, we are.'

'Who have you got on the ground?'

'Jed Carter.'

'Then you tell *Carter* to have something in

fucking writing on my desk by first thing tomorrow morning! What's happened to our backup?'

Joyce seemed to genuinely have no idea. 'We've screwed up. Just leave it with me.'

'As Ops Commander, it's your call, Jo.'

'So, we sit tight at the hotel?' she countered defensively.

'Ivanov won't surface until he knows it's safe to come in. You've let him down once…'

'Kington Square's covered.'

'And what about the Tube station?'

'Don't worry, it's completely watertight,' Joyce said, stooping to pick her handbag off the floor, and mumbled an apology. 'I'm so sorry I wasn't there for him…for Bradley. I let him down.'

'No, you didn't,' he tried assuring her.

Her eyes were moist with tears.

'For Christ's sake, don't beat yourself up about it. One way or another, we've all been there. Besides. you might well have ended up taking a bullet yourself.'

'Trust me; they wouldn't have got the bloody chance. I'd have taken the *bastard* down!'

Spencer held her gaze, a smile hovering on his lips. He knew full well that Joyce was more than capable of doing so; however, he was silently relieved she hadn't been forced to take on Bradley's assassin.

'Have you heard anything from Scotland Yard?' Joyce queried.

'Only that Garvan's forensic team are still

working their way through the flat. We both know it was a professional hit. I'm not expecting them to find anything too worthwhile. I'd be surprised if his killer's left any trace behind him.'

As Joyce stood up to leave, Spencer quietly said to her, 'We'll give it another hour and call it a day.'

'And if he's still a no show?'

Spencer shrugged philosophically. 'Ivanov's a big boy; he knows how to contact us.'

CHAPTER 5

Kensington High Street, South West London

Settling himself on the back seat of the taxi, Ivanov promptly folded his arms and couldn't help but breathe a sigh of relief. He glanced briefly out of the side window, a smile playing about his mouth as the cab drew off, leaving his somewhat frustrated KGB shadow staring helplessly after the taxi at it manoeuvred into the heavy traffic.

The Imperial War Museum was located on the south side of the Thames and in the complete opposite direction to Kington Square. However, Ivanov was all too conscious that he needed to keep on the move before daring to risk zig-zagging a safe route back across the river to the York Hotel for his rendezvous with MI5's spymaster.

It was only after the taxi took a left out of Kensington High Street that Ivanov finally felt able to unclench his fist. He checked the time on his wristwatch before slipping it back on.

Jesus wept, he thought to himself. He was already running almost three-quarters of an hour late.

Ivanov stared almost unseeingly at the endless stream of traffic as the taxi drove along the Cromwell Road, trying to shrug off his doubts. But there was one question churning over in his mind. Would Sir Spencer grant him political asylum?

Successful double agent or not, Ivanov knew there were no guarantees. It was dog eat dog. A dangerous subterranean world, where trust wasn't only hard-gained, it was a rare commodity.

In all fairness, Ivanov had never experienced any serious issues in his dealings with British Intelligence. In fact, far from it. But he'd always put that down to Bradley, his unconsciously suave, astute, and self-deprecating MI5 handler. Right from the start, Bradley was someone Ivanov had felt able to deal with and was totally at ease in his presence. Where the hell was he? Why hadn't he been on the end of the line? It had never happened before. Perhaps he was worrying unnecessarily. Why should today be any different from any other? Well, for a start, it wasn't every day that the head of MI5 answered a handler's telephone number.

Ivanov still tried telling himself that everything would be okay, but his thoughts turned full circle again.

⊰⊱

The black cab crossed Lambeth Bridge over the gun-metal grey Thames and past the London Palace of the Archbishops of Canterbury, with its impressive ancient crenelated gatehouse toward the War Museum.

At a T-junction along Lambeth Road, they suddenly shot across a set of lights before the cabbie did a sharp U-turn against the on-coming traffic and pulled up outside the park gates leading to the grand porticoed museum entrance. Ivanov paid his fare, and thanking the driver, he handed over a generous tip.

He stood back from the kerb a moment watching the taxi move off again into the traffic, before slowly turning to gaze up at the vast copper-domed War Museum. Shortly after his posting to London, Ivanov had accompanied the Soviet Ambassador to the opening of a new exhibition about the siege of Stalingrad by the Nazis. It had made a lasting impression on him.

Since that first visit, he had come to know the surrounding area quite well and had returned with his wife on several occasions. Afterward, they would often end up enjoying a drink, or two, at the Three Stags pub on the corner of Kennington Road.

Hurriedly letting the memory go, Ivanov pivoted around and headed for a nearby zebra crossing. He waited for the traffic to stop before darting over the road.

Lambeth North Underground Station was no more than a few minutes' walk away from the museum; Ivanov was planning on taking the Tube to Kington Square. But he wasn't quite sure how many times he'd have to change lines.

At the ticket office, he paid his fare with the last remains of his small change before confirming his route with the clerk.

The old wooden-floored lift clanked noisily down the steep shaft into the bowels of the unprepossessing station. Juddering to a halt, the metal gate slowly concertinaed open, leading the way onto the two Bakerloo Line platforms. Following the signage, he made his way to the rather dreary northbound platform.

A handful of people were already on the platform awaiting the arrival of the next train. Old habits die hard, and instinctively, he checked them out. A woman was sitting on a slatted wooden bench with a young child beside her. Perhaps the girl's grandmother? Further along the platform, an old man wearing a flat cap was shuffling impatiently to and fro. Beyond him were two smartly dressed men huddled in deep conversation.

Relaxing slightly, his gazed strayed idly across the rail line toward a large poster advertising a new Noel Coward musical called *Sail Away*, starring some actress called Elaine Stritch. Ivanov had no idea who she was, but then again, his experience of musical theatre was, at best, sketchy; it was far more Tasha's department than his.

Feeling a sudden warm breeze flooding the

platform, followed by the unmistakable sound of an approaching Tube train, Ivanov re-checked his ticket before carefully placing it inside his wallet.

Two stops down the line at Embankment Station, Ivanov got off the train and began negotiating his way toward the Circle Line. Some ten minutes later, he emerged at Kington Square.

Taking in his surroundings, he cautiously started to make his way across the large garden square to the York Hotel. Although he had taken every conceivable precaution to shake off his Soviet tail, Ivanov's throat was dry—he could scarcely swallow—and his stomach was knotted with anxiety.

CHAPTER 6

York Hotel, Kington Square
South West London

After a brisk walk across the pretty garden square, with its well-manicured lawns and colourful flower beds, Ivanov stood for a moment outside the York Hotel, gazing up the intricate moulding and decorative carving. He took a step forward, acknowledging the concierge's welcome, and entered the hotel through the ornate revolving doors.

Once inside, he swiftly took stock of the swish chandeliered foyer and ornate mahogany panelling, before his attention finally settled on the familiar figure of MI5's spymaster seated in a high-backed armchair, a folded newspaper in one hand and a pen poised in the other.

Spencer glanced toward his double agent; he looked grey, anxious. A slight hint of recognition passing between them. As instructed, Ivanov continued walking through the foyer to the rear exit leading onto Mercer Street.

Watching Ivanov's progress across the lobby, Spencer reattached the top of his fountain pen and casually slipped it inside his suit jacket. He set the newspaper down on the coffee table and paused just long enough to receive the final okay that it was safe to move off from one of Joyce's operatives who'd followed Ivanov across the Square.

Outside the hotel, Spencer caught up with Ivanov and fell in beside him. His agent muttered an apology for running late.

'There's really no need to apologise,' Spencer assured him.

'It was good of you to wait so long.'

'Why wouldn't I?'

Ivanov thanked him.

'So, how many of your hounds did you manage to pick up on?'

'Only the one,' Ivanov confessed, a little awkwardly.

Spencer didn't respond.

'Your people *must* have noticed he was a little too obvious...and wanted to be seen.'

'Of course, we did. The trouble is, Alexei, in my experience, the KGB always hunt in packs. There's rarely a lone *wolf*. It's not their style.'

His observation elicited a reluctant smile from Ivanov. 'Nor yours. It's a trait we would appear to share.'

Spencer didn't counter him.

'Then, you must know I'm clean?'

'What do you think?'

'I'm guessing if I weren't, you'd have pulled the plug by now.'

Spencer blew out a plume of smoke. His silence was response enough.

'So, where are you taking me?'

'To Peel Street.'

Ivanov visibly relaxed. It was a place he knew well. MI5 owned a safe flat on the street. During his lunch breaks from the Embassy, he would often meet up there with Bradley.

While the venues were, for obvious reasons, a moveable feast, security issues aside, by mutual consent, the format of their meetings had soon developed into a set routine. Ivanov would arrive at the designated rendezvous armed with a selection of classified documents concealed in a full-length poacher's pocket sewn into the lining of his jacket. Their conversations were then tape-recorded, allowing Bradley time to photograph the top-secret documents. The written transcripts would then be drawn up at MI5's HQ. Their lunchtime meetings also allowed Ivanov just enough time to return them to the Embassy without the clerks suspecting the documents had been removed from the building.

To begin with, Bradley had suggested that he might like to consider smuggling a camera into the Embassy and photo everything in-situ. He'd shown him a small Minox camera in the shape of a slender cigarette lighter. Although Ivanov agreed it was a pretty impressive piece of kit, he had dismissed the idea out of hand, considering it was way too risky. It was still a decision he stood by.

Crossing over Mercer Street, they began heading down toward Grosvenor Drive when a black Rover drew up alongside them. Spencer gently nudged Ivanov's arm and indicted to stop. Leaning forward, he opened the rear door and ushered him inside.

'Get in, Alexei, quick as you can.'

As Ivanov eased across the plush back seat, allowing Spencer to join him, he certainly couldn't help noticing the attractive blonde at the wheel. A frisson of surprise entered his expression. Ivanov instinctively shot Spencer a quizzical glance, intending to voice his surprise to find a woman in charge of their getaway car, but had second thoughts.

Sensing his unease, Spencer allowed it to ride and offered the nervous Russian a cigarette.

'May I ask you a question, Sir Spencer?' Ivanov asked readily accepting the proffered cigarette.

'Yes, why not. Fire away.'

'Where's Blackdown?' he queried, his voice tinged with urgency.

Spencer handed him a lighter. 'I'm afraid there's really no easy way of telling you, Alexei. Besides, it'll be all over the front pages soon enough.' He took a long draw on his freshly lit cigarette. 'I'm afraid Bradley's dead.'

Ivanov twisted round on the backseat to face him,

his eyes darting warily. When he finally managed to speak, his words were barely audible. '*Dead*! What happened...was there some kind of accident?'

Spencer screwed up his face before saying drily, 'I suppose you could argue that one shot might be construed an accident, but two...well...'

'Are you able to tell me how it happened?'

'He was murdered this morning.'

'Where?'

'At his flat shortly before you contacted the Office.'

'I'm so sorry, Bradley was a *good* man,' Ivanov apologised.

'Yes, he was,' Spencer responded, seemingly without a shred of emotion.

From all Ivanov knew of Bradley, he wasn't a hugely experienced field man and probably wouldn't have stood a chance up against a seasoned professional KGB officer.

Ivanov finally understood why Spencer had decided to fill the breach. With Bradley down and fearing MI5's top double agent was in danger of being liquidated, he'd taken personal control of the situation. Ivanov felt flattered MI5's Director General had descended from his ivory tower, but at the same time, he was still faintly alarmed by his decision to intervene directly.

Ivanov gazed distractedly out of the car. His mind was all over the place, as random thoughts, like snapshots, entered his head. There'd once been a time in his life when loyalty to the KGB and his country was unwavering. How many years ago now did it all start to unravel steadily? When did his blind and total allegiance to Mother Russia slowly begin to ebb and flow? Until the point where he found himself grappling not only with his conscience, but with everything he had been brought up to believe in. In many ways, it all seemed like a lifetime away.

Promotion within had provided an opportunity to travel and witness first-hand the supposed evil and decadence of Western society. Shortly after his first overseas posting to Paris, the contrast with the Soviet Union wasn't only stark but ultimately also unavoidable. Later on, he'd found himself increasingly comparing the freedoms and prosperity in both Paris, and then London, to the often-harsh grinding reality of day-to-day life behind the Iron Curtain.

But despite his newfound status in the West, Ivanov could never quite understand why his vast, bare floorboard offices were practically empty and had such tiny desks. Their walls lined with the usual obligatory black and white photos of past leaders; however, on Khrushchev's orders, Stalin's image had been expunged.

It was, perhaps, a minor niggle, but somehow only served to highlight the stark differences between Moscow and his newfound freedom.

However, the defining moment in his life had come after the first concrete blocks of the wall dividing East and West Berlin were cemented in place. It had been almost a year ago now, but the wall had somehow shredded his last illusions and confirmed his disenchantment with communism and all it stood for. That coercion, rather than consent, lay at the heart of the Soviet regime. The imposing guarded walls dividing Berlin had witnessed increasing violence meted out to anyone, young or old, who tried to escape the yoke of repression.

Any opposition was, without exception, ruthlessly stifled in all the Soviet Union's satellite states. Intimidation, imprisonment, and even assassination were consequences to anyone who dared to step out of line. Neither the method or means of suppression mattered particularly; the only certainty was that Moscow's message and rule were tantamount. Therefore, resistance was futile and would be crushed without the slightest shred of mercy.

In many ways, his time in Paris and, more recently, in London as the supposed head of the Trade Delegation had been one of sharp contrasts and occasionally tinged with bouts of irony. His often-well-meaning idealistic left-wing contacts and agents viewed communist philosophy as some sort of unattainable utopian ideal of social equality. All the while, Ivanov had only ever dreamed of breaking free and the ability to make a new life in the West. But it was a decision which had come at enormous personal cost, for both his family and now unfortunately for Bradley as well.

CHAPTER 7

Peel Street, South West London

After leaving Grosvenor Drive, it wasn't long before Ivanov had only a vague idea where they were. Each of the streets started to look much like another. Despite his initial misgivings, the attractive blonde at the wheel appeared to be doing a pretty competent job of *provenka*, or, as the British and Americans preferred to call it, *dry-cleaning* a safe route to give any unwanted surveillance the slip. Ivanov was quietly impressed. She was certainly experienced.

Forty minutes into their journey, he started recognising their surroundings and knew they were only a short drive away from Peel Street.

Drawing up outside, a purpose-built apartment block, their back-up vehicle swept past them and parked a short distance along the road. They remained seated in the car with the engine idling over, just in case, until an MI5 officer approached the vehicle and gave a surreptitious thumbs-up that they were good to go.

So far, everything had gone according to plan. The Rover's engine was finally switched off, and much to Ivanov's surprise, the attractive blonde not only escorted them inside the building, but joined them in the safe flat.

Sensing his curiosity, Spencer must have decided it was probably about time he introduced him to Joyce Leader.

She extended a well-manicured hand, but hers wasn't a name he recognised.

With the pleasantries over, Joyce's eyes held his a second with more than just a hint of challenge in them, before unhurriedly settling herself down on a brocaded three-seater sofa.

'Would you care for a drink, Alexei?' Spencer asked.

It was almost akin to asking the Pope whether he prayed or not.

'Yes…yes, please.'

Spencer turned to open a wooden cabinet lined with an array of bottles. In the bottom right-hand corner, a small American refrigerator had been installed.

'Chilled vodka?' he asked, glancing over his shoulder.

Thanking him, Ivanov took to an armchair.

Spencer fished out three cut-glass tumblers from the cabinet. 'Gin and tonic, Jo?'

'Just as long as you go easy on the tonic.'

'Christ, Jo, I wouldn't think of short-changing you! It'd be more than my life was worth!' He laughed.

Waiting for his drink, Ivanov leaned back in the armchair, slowly re-assessing the room. It had been a few weeks since his last meeting with Bradley at the flat. There had been one or two minor changes to the décor. The somewhat clunky, wooden coffee table had been replaced by a modern version with spindly faux brass legs; and above the imposing fireplace was a rural landscape, where once had hung a rather nondescript portrait of some long-forgotten aristocrat in Georgian attire. Neither were particularly to his liking.

Spencer handed out their drinks before deciding on a malt whisky for himself. 'So, Alexei, where are we? What the hell's been going on?' he asked, placing the top back on the bottle.

'Forgive me; I'd have thought it was pretty obvious by now...My cover's blown. Why else would Bradley have been murdered? *I need to come in!*' Ivanov rasped desperately.

Their prized Soviet double agent wasn't a man given to panic easily.

'Why didn't you mention you were in trouble to Bradley?'

'Because I wasn't sure, *that's why!*' Ivanov took a

slug of vodka. 'You must know the surveillance team is fresh blood…imports from Moscow Central!'

Spencer inclined his head slightly in agreement.

Ivanov started fidgeting with his glass. 'There's something else.'

'Go on.'

'I'm being recalled to Moscow.'

Spencer took a slow, appreciative sip of his whisky. He hadn't seen that one coming, and perhaps, more importantly, British Intelligence had failed to pick up on his recall. But why? Up until now, Spencer had assumed their interception of the Embassy's cables was all but watertight. But, somehow, Ivanov's recall had slipped through their intelligence net.

'Have you discussed it with anyone at the Embassy?'

Ivanov rolled his eyes in frustration. 'What difference does it make whether I have or not?'

'It does to me.'

'If you must know, I discussed it with my boss, Demetri Smolin.' He sniffed his name as if there was a distinctly unpleasant smell under his nose.

'And what did he have to say?'

'What do you think! He gave me some yarn or another about an offer of promotion that it seemed genuine enough, and I was probably reading way too much into it!' In an effort to keep the contempt off his face, Ivanov took another large gulp of vodka.

'Then again, Demetri has always been a bloody bad liar. I can smell it a mile off!'

Try as he might, Spencer couldn't entirely take the look of doubt off his face. The Soviets tended to view overseas postings as something of a double-edged sword. It was deemed to be a necessary evil, one which exposed their senior diplomats and KGB officers alike to the risk of contamination from the "supposed" abundant excesses of capitalism.

Perceived risks aside, Ivanov had already had one very successful posting to Paris under his belt and was now only a few months into his appointment as the Trade Secretary to London. A sudden change of plan from the KGB's HQ at Moscow Central was, at best, unlikely. They just didn't work that way.

'You never know Alexei, perhaps you're destined for greater things, after all. Maybe we've missed something.' He smirked.

Ivanov wrinkled up his face in disbelief, emitting a deep-throated chuckle. 'Well, *my friend,* there was a time when that was a very serious possibility. But as we know, Comrade Vasiliev only surrounds himself with his *own* people...officers he can manipulate and use to his advantage.'

Comrade Dima Vasiliev was the current head of the KGB. There was certainly no love lost between them. As young men, they had trained and occasionally worked alongside each other in the field. However, after spectacularly screwing up a major Soviet operation during the mid-fifties in

South America, Vasiliev had apparently destroyed his future career prospects.

He had been subsequently hauled back to Moscow to face the music. Such was his disgrace within the Soviet Intelligence Service; he was destined to see out what remained of his career in some godforsaken backwater. Siberia had been mentioned, but many of his colleagues had suggested that, as far as they were concerned, it still wasn't far enough away from Moscow.

Ivanov had once remarked disparagingly that if Vasiliev had accidentally stepped into a puddle, he'd still have been out of his depth.

Disgraced or not, Vasiliev still had one final ace up his sleeve, and one even the combined might of the KGB and the governing Politburo had found themselves unable to counteract. All too acutely aware, his career was on a sharp terminal trajectory, the wily Vasiliev had swiftly proposed to his young and somewhat impressionable girlfriend. Their relationship could be counted in weeks, rather than months. In the grand scheme of things, Vasiliev wasn't exactly the greatest catch. Fearing the disgraced KGB officer was merely using their daughter to save his neck, the girl's parents had brought pressure to bear not only on their smitten daughter, but also on Vasiliev to end the relationship.

Fortunately, for the increasingly desperate Vasiliev, the girl's tears and protestations had eventually won the day. Her powerful uncle had finally given in to her heartfelt pleas and sanctioned their wedding. Marriage to Anna, the niece of Nikita Khrushchev, the Soviet leader, provided Vasiliev not only the patronage he had always craved, but it also meant his future was ensured and, much to the chagrin of his intelligence colleagues, now entirely bulletproof.

To this day, Vasiliev was still driven by bitterness and contempt for his old rival, blaming Ivanov for failing to back him up over their South American operation. The reality was somewhat different. It was Vasiliev who had screwed up their joint mission to assassinate a leading politician who had fallen foul of Moscow by embedding himself too closely with the CIA.

Not only was their target still alive and kicking after bodging the assassination, but Vasiliev had also been placed under arrest. If it hadn't been for Ivanov's quick thinking to bribe his prison guards, he'd have spent the rest of his life languishing in a squalid South American jail. The diplomatic fallout had certainly caused ripples, but greasing the palms of corrupt politicians had also helped to smooth matters over.

Spencer's gaze idly drifted back toward Ivanov as he restlessly moved away from the armchair and began pacing back and forth, immersed in thought like a frustrated caged animal.

'If you were a betting man, Sir Spencer, what do you think the chances are of Vasiliev welcoming me with open arms to Moscow Central and offering me a promotion?'

'Realistically?'

'Yes.'

'Well, I'd say even before the surveillance stuff kicked off, at best, no more than fair to middling.'

Ivanov stopped pacing the room and laughed. 'You're far too generous. Trust me; there's more chance of hell freezing over than Comrade Vasiliev inviting me to become one of his *henchmen*.' He grunted derisively.

Spencer stared at him, speculatively. 'No, I suppose you're right.'

'I can't understand why he bothered dispatching his people to London. I was due to return home on leave at the end of the month. Why not have me arrested in Moscow?' he added, frustrated.

Spencer agreed with him that it didn't add up.

'So, we have to ask ourselves, why has he moved now? The only thing I can come up with is that something or someone has forced his...'

Joyce cut across him mid-sentence. 'Can you tell us why your wife returned home unexpectedly last week?'

Ivanov turned sharply, irritated by her interruption. 'Because we were told Tasha's father was gravely ill.'

'And was he?'

He threw his arms out in an expansive, exasperated gesture. 'Please don't play games with me, Miss Leader! You must know by now it was nothing more than a ruse to part us...to trap Tasha and our children in Moscow.'

Joyce coolly slipped a cigarette between her lips, turned on a lighter, and carefully played the flame against the tip. 'Have you managed to speak to your wife?'

'You know damn well I *have*!'

She pursed her lips, slowly blowing out a cloud of smoke. 'And how did she seem?'

The flintiness in his expression suddenly boiled over. '*Miss Leader*, may I suggest you might try reading MI5's transcripts of our conversations. It'd save all of us a great deal of time and effort!'

Her eyes calmly swept over him. She was almost beginning to appreciate why Bradley had complained he'd had his work cut out running their prized, albeit volatile, double agent. Bradley had taken on the mantle with considerable trepidation. Whatever way you look at it, it hadn't been a smooth ride for him. But with a combination of sheer dogged determination and innate charm, he had eventually contrived to win Ivanov over and gain his trust.

Joyce didn't rise to the bait; there was no point in doing so. As a result of her silence, Ivanov appeared faintly awkward. For Christ's sake, the last thing he could afford was to alienate them. It hadn't been his intention to offend either of them, and he decided to soften his tone.

'What you have to understand, Miss Leader,' he

51

said measuredly, 'is that the KGB has always excelled at mind games. But Comrade Vasiliev has taken it to another level altogether. With my family trapped in...' As his words faltered, he turned to face the window.

His cover was blown; the game was up. As far as Moscow was concerned, he was nothing more than a shabby traitor who had sold out his country and would be sentenced to death in absentia.

As a traitor, the status afforded to a senior KGB officer and his family would be withdrawn immediately. He could only hope his decision to keep Tasha in the dark about his spying for the West would provide her with a degree of protection. Besides, how did you begin to hide a secret which permeated every last fibre of your body, let alone share it?

On their arrival, Tasha and the children would have been picked up at the airport by his colleagues and taken under close guard to their flat. Since then, she would have endured several lengthy interrogations, which would have no doubt left her feeling bewildered and angry. Eventually, they'd discover she had nothing to tell, but innocent or not, as the wife of a traitor, she and their wider family would be cast as social pariahs. As the pressure mounted, life would become increasingly difficult for all of them. The only unknown was whether or not Tasha could ever find it within her heart to forgive him. He somehow doubted it.

For all their sakes, Ivanov knew he couldn't allow his deep-rooted animosity toward Vasiliev to cloud his judgement and needed to choose his words wisely. To try and keep both his brain and mouth in gear.

'You have to understand,' he said at length, 'that Vasiliev's marriage to our *esteemed* leader's niece meant he was no longer subject to the same KGB rules and regulations governing the rest of us. He was suddenly immune. Above it all. Like Lazarus, his career rose from the dead.'

For all that he'd tried to disguise his feelings, his voice was still edged with vitriol. 'Past wrongs and mistakes were erased from the records. As if the South American operation had never happened. Vasiliev became the man of the future. In fact, within our circle, he was the *only* man of the future. With Khrushchev's patronage, he was promoted above his peer group and,' he smiled cynically, 'his somewhat limited capabilities. You see, promotion is one thing, but Vasiliev also needed to keep a sharp eye on the future, and, more importantly, one without his wife's uncle as leader.'

A slight smile again started playing about his mouth. 'With rumours circulating about the old man, it's pretty much open season now in Moscow. But...I'll give him his due, Vasiliev is nothing but a survivor. He's wasted little time in settling real or perceived old scores.' Ivanov paused to take a breath, before adding sarcastically, 'It's taken a while, but then again, it's a *very* long list!'

'Well, so far, he seems to be doing a pretty good job,' Joyce observed dryly.

Ivanov smiled a sad, cynical smile.

'Didn't he once threaten to string you up by a certain part of your anatomy?'

The memory forced Ivanov to chuckle. 'Yes, it was after our return to Moscow from South America. At the time, I brushed it off. Right now, it doesn't seem quite so laughable.'

'No, I guess it doesn't,' she sympathised.

'You have to understand Vasiliev's ultimate ambition is to succeed his wife's uncle.'

A look of doubt crossed Spencer's face. '*Really*? Are you being serious?'

'I've underestimated the bastard once. I won't make the same mistake twice!'

Over the last eighteen months, Spencer knew there had been rumblings of discontent within the Kremlin about Khrushchev's future. As he'd grown older, he seemed not quite so sure-footed. There were signs that his tight-fisted grip was becoming a little less secure and erratic in his actions. Consequently, the hyenas were slowly, but inevitably, starting to circle their prey. In hindsight, perhaps the old man's patronage of Vasiliev wasn't to be entirely unexpected.

Even before Vasiliev's appointment to head up the Security Service, Khrushchev and his inner circle had fallen increasingly under closer scrutiny, with the ever-present and the real threat of the KGB using microphones to spy upon them. Vasiliev's appointment had at least temporarily, or so they hoped, allayed many of their justifiable fears.

While the in-fighting remained ongoing as the various factions jockeyed for power, Spencer suspected Vasiliev was all too conscious that Khrushchev's successor might well view his closeness to the old regime as little more than toxic.

Noting Ivanov's glass was empty, Spencer poured another large vodka.

'If it's any consolation, Alexei,' he said, handing it to him, 'our European Stations haven't picked up on anything out of the ordinary coming from Moscow Central.'

A shadow of disappointment crossed the Russian's face, but he wasn't surprised. 'Do you think it's possible the same Judas betrayed Anatoly Mirsky?' He cupped the glass in his hands. 'Have the CIA come up with anything?'

'It's early days, Alexei.'

A month ago, Mirsky had been working as a double agent for the Americans. Unaware of his impending fate, he had returned to Moscow on a routine duty visit only to discover his cover was blown. A week later, he was tried and convicted of spying for an enemy State.

Shortly after his execution, rumours soon began circulating that someone operating at the heart of the CIA or closer to home in British Intelligence was behind his betrayal.

'I think we're all agreed that Mirsky was handed to the KGB on a plate!' Ivanov announced sourly.

While Spencer had no intention of being drawn into speculating who was to blame, he assured Ivanov the hunt for their mole hadn't run out of steam, and that both the CIA and British Intelligence were in the midst of an intense investigation. It was a deliberately opaque response, but no more than Ivanov had expected. All the same, he thanked him.

'The trouble is, Sir Spencer, from where *I'm* sitting, I only have so much time to outrun a bullet, and whoever outed me also has Bradley's blood on their hands.'

'It doesn't matter what I believe, Alexei. I only work on hard facts.'

'Then I just hope to God, Miss Leader, you're pretty handy with a pistol!'

Joyce found his comment faintly patronising and assumed if she'd been a man, it wouldn't probably have even entered his head to question her ability. Then again, over the years, she'd met his type before and ignored the jibe. She didn't have to prove herself and certainly not to the likes of Ivanov.

Joyce shot Spencer a knowing smile, and he merely echoed her smile.

Noting the informal exchange between them, the message was crystal clear. Ivanov knew he'd overstepped the mark and shouldn't have had the temerity to question the ice-cool blonde's ability. He guessed Spencer's faith in her was validation enough and wasn't up for discussion.

CHAPTER 8

Special Forces Club
Knightsbridge, South West London

The Assistant Commissioner's chauffeur-driven car pulled out of Scotland Yard onto the Victoria Embankment. They followed the course of the Thames upriver to Chelsea Bridge Road, where it took a right turn and then drove across Sloane Square, heading toward a quiet, elegant street in Knightsbridge near Harrods.

The chauffeur pulled to a stop outside what had once been an imposing Edwardian townhouse. There was really nothing to distinguish it from any of the other palatial residences in the surrounding area.

Luke Garvan's driver glanced over his left shoulder. 'Do you want me to wait here for you, sir?'

'No, I could be some time. I'll give you a call later

when I've finished. You might as well get yourself back to the Yard and grab a bite to eat.'

'Thanks, Guv,' he said, with genuine gratitude. 'Let's hope it's not a late one.'

'Yes, so do I,' came the weary response.

Garvan let himself out of the car and headed up the shallow porticoed steps, pushing the bell. Adjusting the knot of his tie, he waited a moment, before pressing it again. Eventually, the heavy black-painted door was opened by a rather well-dressed, athletic-looking man of a certain age. It crossed Garvan's mind he was probably ex-Special Forces and was, perhaps, in his mid-to-late fifties, but then again, he could have been slightly older.

Garvan announced himself and proffered his police ID.

'That won't be necessary, sir, please come in. We've been expecting you. I'm Geordie,' he said by way of introduction, extending his hand in welcome. 'If you could just sign the visitor's register, sir, I can then take you through to the bar.' He closed the door behind them.

'Yes, of course.'

The reception desk was nestled in what could only be described as little more than a cubby hole tucked beside the entrance. Although Garvan had been a close friend of Spencer's for well over twenty years, an invite to the Special Forces Club was surprisingly a first for him. He felt intrigued, if not a little alarmed, by the invitation.

Their usual watering hole was the Naval and Military Club in Piccadilly, opposite Green Park. It was known locally as the "In & Out" on account of the prominent signs displayed on the building's separate vehicle entrance and exit.

On first impressions, in comparison, the Special Forces Club seemed surprisingly understated, but then again, it was somewhat more exclusive than any other London club.

A slightly faded oriental rug occupied the dark oak flooring, and four comfortable chairs, which had all seen far better days, were scattered randomly about the wide hallway. There was an almost shabby gentility about the place; it was more like a home away from home, rather than a prestigious, expensive club.

After signing himself in the visitor's register, Geordie ushered Garvan up the red-carpeted staircase, where photographs lined the wall. They were the faces of the men and women who had served with the Special Operations Executive during the war or, as it became more popularly known, the SOE; the remainder belonged to members of the SAS.

Each of the framed photos was inset with a metal nameplate and a brief annotation, scripted with their fate behind enemy lines and the date of their death. Garvan couldn't help but stop mid-stride and read a couple of the inscriptions.

Geordie half-turned on the landing and smiled back down.

'I'm sorry,' Garvan apologised.

'There's no need, sir, take as long as you like.'

Garvan looked up at him with a throwaway gesture. 'It's okay. I'll check them out later on.'

They continued up a further flight and then down a fairly dark corridor leading to a cosy bar area. Inside, there were three young men huddled together around a heavily beer-stained table, deep in conversation. His arrival barely registered, although they politely acknowledged him with a fleeting nod but no more.

Over by the window, Spencer was stretched out in an armchair facing the door and raised his hand in greeting. Hauling himself out of the chair, he stepped forward, thanking Garvan for coming at short notice.

Geordie hovered attentively until they were both seated. 'Right, gentlemen, what can I get you to drink?'

'I'll have my usual, thank you, and I'm guessing a light ale for the Assistant Commissioner.'

Garvan inclined his head. 'Do you have any Bass?'

'Of course, we do, sir. Would you like a half or a pint?'

'It's been a long day, Geordie; you'd better make it a pint.'

'I'll be back with you in a minute,' he said, heading across to the bar.

'I'm sorry, I know you've already got enough on your plate.'

'I really wouldn't bother your head about it,'

Garvan mused, carefully taking in his surroundings. 'You've been keeping this place under your belt, haven't you?'

'Yes…yes, I suppose I have.'

'So, why the invite?' Garvan asked curiously.

Spencer took a while considering his reply. 'I usually only ever use the Club to come and relax… to be perfectly frank with you, it never seemed quite appropriate to discuss business here.'

'What's changed your mind?'

He breathed wearily. 'I guess it's probably just about the only place left I can guarantee if we're overheard, nothing will ever get out.'

Garvan looked slightly disconcerted and shot him a quizzical look. In the past, there had never been any particular security issues surrounding their meeting at the Naval and Military Club. They tended to be strictly off the record, allowing them a certain leeway and as much operational freedom as was reasonably possible.

Alternatively, why hadn't he opted for Scotland Yard or MI5? There had to be a reason.

'What the hell's going on, Spence?' he asked, warily.

Spencer slipped a cigarette between his lips and began playing the lighter against the tip. 'How's the investigation going at Bradley's flat?' he said, side-stepping the question.

Garvan heaved his shoulders slightly. 'Why are you asking *me*?'

'Because you're in charge of the bloody investigation, Luke, that's why!'

'I'm surprised Joyce hasn't briefed you already,' he stated, acid creeping into his voice.

The bitterness in his response wasn't entirely unexpected.

'Yes, she has,' Spencer said flatly.

Returning from the bar with their drinks, Geordie silenced their conversation. They thanked him as he padded off discreetly.

'How are things going between you two?' Spencer queried, almost as a throwaway line.

Garvan couldn't entirely hide his irritation. 'You mean with Joyce?'

'Yes.'

'Are you joking?'

'Well, I know you'd called off the wedding.'

'I think you'll find it was Joyce who called off the wedding!'

'I didn't know whether you'd managed to patch things up.'

'If we had, then I'm sure *you'd* have been the first to know.' Garvan smirked.

Spencer couldn't help feeling a twinge of guilt. His decision to reactivate Joyce's file at the beginning of the year hadn't only caused an unexpected rift. It had eventually proved to be the final nail in their frequently volatile relationship. Stifling his initial response, Spencer ended up mumbling an apology of sorts for inadvertently creating a fissure between them.

'I wouldn't bother,' he said dismissively.

Although Garvan had long since valued Spencer's friendship and advice, in the past, they'd often found themselves crossing swords—each stubbornly fighting their own corner and unwilling to compromise.

There was a brief, awkwardness between the two men before Spencer felt compelled to break the silence.

'Are your people still at the flat?

Garvan glanced down at his wristwatch. 'I should imagine they might be starting to wind things up by now until the morning.'

'Do you know if they've come with anything?'

'Well, nothing to speak off. The coroner's done his bit and has allowed the body to be removed. I'll have an interim report from Damien Jacks tomorrow.'

Spencer arched his brows questioningly.

'He's the new head of forensics,' Garvan explained. 'Don't worry; I'll keep you posted.'

'Thanks.'

'Which reminds me,' he said, taking a large draught of ale.

Spencer looked at him searchingly and waited.

'What the hell was Joyce doing at Bradley's flat?'

'Joyce was there. Why didn't you ask her yourself?'

Garvan rolled his eyes. 'Of course I bloody did!'

'And?'

'What do you think?

'I don't know, you tell me.'

'She did her usual ruddy trick of stonewalling me and suggested in her own sweet way that I really needed to talk things through with you. I suppose she was under orders to keep things tight,' he added pointedly.

Spencer couldn't deny it.

'Besides,' Garvan sneered, slumping back in his chair, 'Joyce didn't exactly hang around too long after I arrived at the flat.'

'Why, did you expect her to?'

'Not necessarily,' came the deadpan reply. 'So, what have you got for me?'

Spencer began toying thoughtfully with the cigarette between his fingers, a faint grimace on his features, passing for a smile. 'They'd arranged to meet for breakfast at his flat.'

Garvan looked genuinely surprised. 'I didn't even know she knew him.'

'Well…there's really no reason why you should have.'

Garvan screwed up his face in something approaching despair. 'Christ, you're not going to tell me it was Jo who shot the poor sod, *are you*?'

'Good God, no!' Spencer said, sounding faintly horrified. 'Bradley was one of us; he was working for MI5.'

'He was *what*?' Garvan said in disbelief.

As the head of Special Branch, Garvan was directly responsible for Prime Minister Gerry

Hawley's security. Bradley's closeness to the PM, or so he had been led to believe, was a long-standing headache for the Security Services. Although hugely successful and influential, Bradley's often nefarious and convoluted business deals hadn't always stood up to too much scrutiny.

Although, there was much to be admired about the man Bradley had invariably sailed pretty close to the wind. He was a self-made millionaire and legendary entrepreneur who had made his first fortune in the textile industry. Five years ago, he had decided to diversify his business empire by buying up a string of exclusive West End nightclubs and restaurants. It had proved an astute move.

A New Yorker by birth, Bradley's parents had divorced when he was five years old. After separating, his English mother had decided to return home with him to be closer to her family in London. The young, academically bright boy had subsequently spent the school holidays with his American father and, by all accounts, had continued to retain a close relationship with both his parents and step-siblings.

Security issues aside, loyally defending his friend, the Prime Minister had always brushed Garvan's concerns aside, arguing he'd never allow Special Branch or British Intelligence to dictate his personal life.

Officially, he'd drawn a line; it wasn't up for discussion. However, the PM's stance had done little, if anything, to quell the endless speculation surrounding their friendship. As far as Garvan was concerned, Bradley's involvement with MI5 had merely fanned the flames of an already awkward situation.

He was also struggling to get his head around the idea that Bradley—*of all people*—had been considered MI5 material. Let alone end up as the victim of a possible professional hit.

'Why the hell didn't you tell me he was working for you? On second thought, just keep me out of it!'

'Luke, it wasn't that I didn't want to…'

'Where have I heard that line before?'

'Bradley was out on a limb.'

'I'm sure he was.'

'We needed to cover his back.'

'Then it didn't bloody work, did it,' Garvan said sarcastically.

'It was complicated.'

'Give me a time when it hasn't been complicated.'

'Bradley wasn't officially on the books.'

'And what's that supposed to mean? Is there such a thing as a part-time spy?'

'As I said, it's a little complicated.'

'How long had he been working for you?'

'Not that long,' Spencer responded obliquely.

Garvan figured it wasn't worth pressing him. The damage was done. 'I just don't get why you'd risk employing him.'

'Think about it. What did Bradley have going for him?'

'I don't know…money, contacts?' He shrugged indifferently.

'Well, he certainly had both in spades. I know you've always thought he was little more than a glorified social climber.'

'He was,' Garvan said bluntly. 'Why else did he bother getting his mitts on the PM?'

'They fed off each other. It was a two-way street. Bradley had all the powerful business and social contacts the PM craved. On the back of that, yes, Bradley basked in his reflected glory, but like it or not, they somehow ended up as close friends.'

Garvan accepted, albeit reluctantly, he might have a point.

'I'm not denying Bradley didn't have issues.'

'That's one way of looking at it.'

Spencer smiled slightly in response. 'Dodgy or not, we needed his help.'

'Because of the Prime Minister?'

'I know you won't believe me, but that wasn't the main reason I targeted him.'

Garvan screwed up his face in scorn. 'You're right, Spence, I don't!'

'I'd be lying if his friendship with the PM didn't have its uses.'

'So, the PM had no idea whatsoever Bradley was batting for MI5?'

'No…well…'

'Does he know *now*?' Garvan asked tentatively.

'As of an hour ago.'

'And *you* briefed him?'

'Yes, I did.'

'Then I'm guessing it went down like a lead balloon!'

'Let's just say, by the time I left No.10, he was spitting rivets and bringing my parentage into doubt.' He smirked.

Garvan drained the dregs of his ale. 'The PM aside, what was the hook? I still don't understand why you'd run the risk of approaching Bradley?'

'I needed an in at the Cavalier Club,' he said quietly.

The Cavalier was a discreet club cum restaurant based in the heart of Soho. It was the newest addition to Bradley's growing property portfolio. According to the latest Inland Revenue tax returns, to-date, it was one of his highest earners.

Ever the savvy businessman, Bradley had wanted it to stand out from the crowd. No expense was spared on either the décor or its renowned art collection. Boasting an outstanding restaurant, two bars, and an exclusive nightclub, the Cavalier had swiftly grown to become one of the in-places to be seen in London.

It was also well known the Prime Minister viewed the Cavalier as a haven, somewhere he could retreat to with a degree of anonymity. Not unnaturally, his patronage had ensured its popularity not only amongst his closest political supporters, but also with the Labour Party's left-wing factions and trade unions leaders alike. By default, the Cavalier was also, perhaps somewhat unsurprisingly, targeted time and again by the Soviet Embassy's KGB staff as a lucrative hunting ground to meet and potentially cultivate useful contacts.

For Ivanov, in particular, the Cavalier had proved a successful location for scoping out potential contacts and people they could hopefully influence. It had provided him with some of his best results since his arrival in London. He simultaneously reported back to Moscow. At the same time, he offered MI5 details of UK nationals deemed by the Soviet authorities as either useful contacts – whom he was instructed to cultivate – plus intelligence regarding full-blown agents already working for the KGB, many of whom regularly socialised at the Cavalier.

Spencer accepted, at least on paper, that Bradley was probably one of the very last people on earth you'd have suspected of working for MI5, nor would Moscow Central.

Bradley was viewed as nothing more than a wealthy, vain socialite with money to burn. He was photographed week in week out, the press cuttings were inches deep, and he gave the appearance of being totally open, but he was fundamentally a private person. It was an interesting combination.

'Bradley was loyal and hardworking,' Spencer insisted.

'I still don't get it.'

'Why not?'

'Maybe I'm missing something.'

'Like what?'

'How did you hook him? I guess it can't have been easy.'

'It was a process of elimination.'

'Was it…tax evasion?'

'No, it wasn't. He's always been entirely upfront about his tax affairs. Whether the Inland Revenue like it or not, his accountants haven't actually broken any UK laws; yes, they've sent shed loads of money abroad, but it isn't illegal.'

'But it is a tax dodge!'

'I don't particularly care what it is. If I could afford the very best accountants, I'd hope they'd do the same thing for me!'

'So, how exactly did you hook him?'

'I suppose you could say, we played on his vanity,' Spencer said thoughtfully. 'I guess he was flattered British Intelligence was interested in him. We set our cards out on the table. As the owner of the Cavalier, it was suggested he was ideally placed to approach our Soviet friends without arousing their suspicion. Besides, he already socialised with them regularly; and more importantly, they already trusted him.'

'You were taking one hell of a risk.'

'It was worth taking, and before you ask, we certainly didn't coerce or pressurize Bradley into doing anything against his will, in fact, far from it. We played it carefully, gave him some space. I didn't want to run the risk of scaring him off.'

'Who recruited him, or need I ask?'

'Joyce made most of the running.'

'Yes, I *bet* she did,' Garvan said waspishly.

Spencer arched his brows questioningly.

'Did she sleep with him?'

'Why on earth would she?'

'You tell me. It wouldn't be the first time, though, would it?' Garvan snorted, acid creeping into his voice.

Spencer let the jibe pass without comment. There was simply no point in rising to the bait. Right now, he needed to try and keep Garvan on-side, but the way things were panning out, it was going to be an uphill struggle.

He decided to change tack and keep Joyce out of the equation by explaining that once they'd Bradley onboard, he had hit on the idea of hosting several small, discreet supper parties at the Cavalier Club.

'For what reason?'

'It was an easy way of getting closer to *certain* people, whom, shall I say…were of particular interest to the Service.'

'You mean, Ivanov?'

'Not just Ivanov, no. We actually ended up handing him quite a long list. In the early days, Ivanov still wasn't quite in the bag. He was teetering, yes, but hadn't yet fully committed. In many respects, it was an easy fix. They already knew each socially from the Club; the supper party's provided Bradley with a discreet way of taking things to another level.'

'And what about the Prime Minister?'

Spencer scowled. 'I'm sorry, what about him?'

'Please don't tell me he was invited to any of Bradley's cosy little get-togethers?'

'No, certainly not!' Spencer almost sounded offended by the suggestion. 'Bradley was always careful. His friendship with the PM was always strictly off-limits.'

'Well, let's hope to God he did!'

'I'm telling you, Bradley was sound,' Spencer snapped irritably.

Garvan shook his head in despair. 'You're living on borrowed time, Spence.'

'One way or another, we all are,' came the deadpan response.

'Go on, then. Tell me why the poor bastard ended up paying with his life.'

Cradling his half-empty glass this way and that between his hands, Spencer took a deep intake of breath. 'During Ivanov's stint in Paris, he'd started to put out feelers to British Intelligence. By the time he had arrived in London, he was still wavering…but wouldn't fully commit himself to become a double agent. Then again, I really can't blame him. His MI6 contact from Paris, Jeff Sawyer, continued to stay in regular touch. They'd meet up occasionally in London. Eventually, when Sawyer had decided the time was right, he let slip that Bradley was in the Service.'

'And how did that go down?'

'Surprisingly well. Mind you, if Ivanov's half as good as we believe him to be, I imagine he saw it coming. Not that he's ever let on, of course.' Resting his empty glass on the table, he held Garvan's eyes a fraction. 'He became Ivanov's handler.'

Garvan shook his head without comment.

'I've kept Bradley's involvement with the Service low-key.'

'Yes, I bet you bloody have! I still don't get why you didn't use someone far more experienced to reel Ivanov in.'

'Well, Sawyer certainly worked hard enough on him in Paris, but he still wouldn't budge. After he arrived in London, Ivanov became my responsibility, and mine alone. I needed a softer line. By the time we decided to make a formal approach, Ivanov had already grown to enjoy Bradley's company. Away from the club, they'd meet up for an occasional drink at the Red Lion pub in Whitehall. Ivanov felt comfortable around him.'

Garvan shrugged. 'So what? After he agreed to come across, you could still have chosen someone else to handle him.'

'In some ways, it was taken out of my hands.'

'That's got to be a first, then!'

'Ivanov didn't want anyone to run him.'

Garvan closed his eyes briefly. 'Like a lamb to the ruddy slaughter. The poor sod didn't stand a chance, did he?'

He'd obviously hit a raw nerve. Spencer's anger,

although unspoken, was palpable. Barely holding his temper in check, he indicated to the bar staff he needed a refill, and a large one this time.

Undeterred, Garvan pressed him. 'Why didn't you warn me off before I arrived at the poor sod's flat this morning?'

'Because I didn't get a chance to, that's why. I was already waist-deep in shit and drowning. Shortly after Joyce raised the alert, Ivanov called the Office, asking for an urgent meeting. Of course, normally, Bradley would have handled everything.'

'Has Ivanov asked for political asylum?'

'Yes, his cover's blown. He's thrown in the towel.'

'Was the timing coincidental?'

'You know, I've never particularly believed in coincidence. But who knows,' Spencer shrugged. 'With Bradley down, I needed to take control and bring him in myself.'

Garvan's face relaxed into a slow, grudging smile. 'I bet that put the wind up the old bugger's sails!'

'I hadn't thought about it, but I daresay it did.'

'Even if his cover has been blown, why on earth would the KGB go to the trouble of taking Bradley out? It doesn't make sense.'

'A warning shot, perhaps, or they wanted to cause maximum embarrassment.'

'You mean, because of the PM?'

'I'm speculating, Luke,' Spencer confessed. 'Who knows, perhaps he'd stumbled across something important, and they needed to silence him.'

'How do you want me to play things with Bradley's family? I understand his father's flying over from the States tomorrow. I assume you'd rather his parents didn't know what he was up to?'

Spencer pulled a face. 'I think it'd be better all-round, *don't you*?

'I guess so.'

'Just tell them you're investigating a possible burglary gone wrong.' Spencer made a throwaway gesture. 'I'm sure you'll think of something, you always do.'

'Yes,' Garvan sighed wearily. 'I had a feeling you'd say that!'

CHAPTER 9

Peel Street, South West London

As a radio played quietly in the background, Ivanov was alone with his thoughts about what was to come. He felt isolated and was reluctant to leave the safe flat, a place he'd come to know well over the last few months during his lunchtime meetings with Bradley.

As someone who had always managed to retain at least a modicum of control over his life, Ivanov was rapidly finding himself not only haunted by past decisions, but perhaps, more importantly, by the uncertainty of the future, which was beginning to fill him with increasing dread.

To his erstwhile KGB colleagues, he was nothing more than a whistle-blower, a traitor to the Motherland. No mercy would be given or expected. Although he'd so far managed to escape their clutches, Ivanov knew it was nothing more than a temporary stay of execution.

There was only one certainty; the KGB would never rest until he was finally six feet under. Bradley's murder wasn't just neatly timed; it also served as a deadly warning that one day he, too, would suffer a similar fate at the hands of Moscow Central.

He wandered over to the living room window and gently tweaked the net curtains, before turning away sharply as the BBC news came back on the air. Bradley's murder, as earlier, was the main headline.

His gaze strayed thoughtfully toward this morning's newspapers scattered across the coffee table. Over breakfast, he'd read each of them in turn, pawing over the grim editorials and a selection of black and white photos of his late friend.

Going public with the news of his death had been given the go-ahead late yesterday afternoon by Prime Minister Hawley, allowing Fleet Street time to ensure the story had made the morning editions. The PM's statement expressed his deep shock on learning of his friend's death, and that his thoughts and prayers were very much with Bradley's family at this difficult time. He also pleaded with the press to allow them time to grieve in private. But, fearing his plea would fall on deaf ears, he had already ordered a police presence to be posted outside Bradley's distraught mother's Surrey home, before they found themselves besieged by journalists.

It was early days, but so far, the coverage had

been mainly sympathetic to both the family and the PM. But, as expected, there were one or two more salacious editorials, the *Daily Mirror* in particular, who wasted little time roping in one of Bradley's supposed girlfriends, who claimed they were engaged to be married. It was the usual dross. MI5 already knew for a fact he hadn't seen the girl for at least six months. But there was mileage to be gained from the interview, increased circulation for the *Mirror*, and fleeting fame of sorts for the attractive young woman, coupled with a nice fat pay cheque from the paper to boot.

Although there was little, as yet, in the way of hard facts, many of the more serious editorials were peppered with a liberal sprinkling of speculation. However, by and large, they were generally just throwing ideas into the mix, probably in the hope of selling a few more copies.

As Joyce's voice cut through his thoughts, Ivanov glanced up from the coffee table.

'I'm afraid, Alexei, we need to leave now,' she said, switching off the radio.

Ivanov puffed out his cheeks in resignation. 'Are we going to the Fort?'

'Do you mean Fort Monkton?'

He nodded.

'No, I'm sorry, Alexi, there's been a change of plan,' Joyce answered briskly.

Ivanov's expression registered surprise. Fort Monkton had started life out as a nineteenth-century

Royal Navy fortress on the south coast of England, but was now a secure training base for Britain's intelligence organisations. The Fort had always been factored into the equation as a bolt hole. Whenever the subject was raised with Bradley about the prospect of his defecting to the West, he always assured him the place was crucial to their initial planning. So, what had happened to alter their plans?

Hurriedly collecting his thoughts, he pressed, 'So where *are* we going?'

'A mews house in London.'

Ivanov arched his brows in surprise. 'Where, exactly?'

'Chelsea.'

In comparison to the Fort, some fancy bloody London mews didn't quite fit the bill.

'I'm sorry, Miss Leader, but have your people really thought this through? I mean...' he ventured.

'I'm afraid it's not my call, Alexei. We'd better get a move on; we're running late as it is,' she cut across him, picking up the car keys off the sideboard.

Outside the apartment block, a small, top of the range MG was waiting for them. After swiftly casting an admiring eye over the sports car, Ivanov instinctively started checking their surroundings in search of their back-up team.

'Get in,' Joyce gestured, and waited until he was settled in the passenger seat before climbing in beside him.

A slow, appreciative smile crossed Ivanov's face

as the MG's engine growled throatily into life, but how she ever managed to drive so skilfully in such vertiginous stilettoes was still quite beyond him.

Ten minutes into their drive, he assumed Joyce was following a pre-set route through a myriad of side-streets to their destination in Chelsea. Pre-planned or not, he wasn't entirely sure whether she was either familiar with the surrounding area or had studied the A to Z of London with a fine-tooth comb.

As they drew up at a set of traffic lights, Ivanov routinely checked out his passenger wing mirror. Jerking an urgent thumb over his shoulder, he turned to her.

'I suppose you do realise we're being followed by a motorbike?'

'Relax, Comrade; he's one of ours,' she said, releasing the handbrake as the lights changed to green.

'Are you sure?'

Joyce coldly returned his gaze. 'What do you think?' she snapped sarcastically.

There was a directness, an almost otherness about her, a certain intensity, Ivanov found fascinating and yet at the same time slightly disturbing.

Joyce swung the sports car around Sloane Square, into the King's Road, past the old Duke of York's Barracks before taking a right into Sumner Place. Their motorbike outrider briefly drew alongside them, inclined his head slightly to her, before shooting off, weaving in and out of the heavy traffic.

They lost sight of him altogether until they arrived at the safe house in the elegant cobbled St Barnabas Mews.

From humble origins as stables and servants' quarters, mews houses were rapidly becoming something of a status symbol across West London. The once abandoned buildings of the wealthy were converted initially during the 1950s into residential homes by a trendy influx of successful racing drivers, such as Stirling Moss, who, for not much money, could live directly above their cars. Since then, they had become the "in-place" to live, attracting a plethora of successful artists, photographers, and actors alike.

By the time they arrived, their motorbike escort had already been given the okay to proceed by the back-up team, located in the house opposite their own. The escort unlocked the black painted wooden coach doors, allowing Joyce to drive straight into the double-spaced garage without stopping outside. Once they were safely inside, the leather clad escort swiftly bolted the doors behind them.

Joyce pulled on the handbrake, switched off the engine, and alighted from the car, her face relaxing into a warm smile.

'Thanks, Jed.'

Easing off his helmet, he shot her a lop-sided grin.

Ivanov gave their well-built escort a long appraising look. He possessed an innate confidence, the stance, the way he conducted himself, like Spencer Hall, reeked of Special Forces. They were the same the world over.

He approached Ivanov and extended his hand in welcome. 'Jed Carter,' he announced, introducing himself.

Ivanov smiled in response.

'Are we ready?' Joyce said to no-one in particular.

Whether they were or not, she headed over to the rear of the garage and up a steep, echoing wrought iron spiral staircase, which led directly into a tastefully decorated and surprisingly spacious contemporary style living room.

There to greet them was a not overly tall, lean, neatly trimmed bearded man, who was introduced by Joyce as Dave Lewis. She explained he was the officer in charge of their back-up team both in the mews and the surrounding area. He'd also been tasked with making all the necessary in-house arrangements before their arrival.

Judging by the slightly bemused expression on Lewis's face, Ivanov couldn't help thinking that stocking up on supplies was a somewhat unexpected add-on to his normal day-to-day duties.

Within the Service, it was common knowledge that Spencer had always made a particular point of looking after Lewis. But no-one knew quite why. He was generally viewed as something of an enigma within British Intelligence circles.

Lewis was an ex-Royal Navy engineer petty officer

by trade, whom Spencer had come across eight years ago. Entirely what he had done for the Service, only Spencer knew. No-one questioned it, but as a result, all knew Lewis was practically untouchable.

On the surface, he came across as a quiet, calm, almost self-effacing man with a ready wit. Perhaps it was his sheer unobtrusiveness and straight talking, which had helped make him such an effective, insightful MI5 officer. Lewis was Spencer's man. His loyalty was a given and, like Joyce, was part of his inner sanctum.

'Is everything okay?' Joyce asked him.

Lewis winked in response. 'It couldn't be better, *ma'am*,' he answered, knowing the term rankled with her.

'Drop the bloody ma'am business, will you!'

'Whatever you say, ma…'

'Just get on with it, *Dave,* and give us the sodding guided tour!'

Lewis proceeded to show them around the mews house. Although he'd obviously been working to a brief, Ivanov still appreciated his eye for detail and thought behind trying to accommodate him.

There was an entirely new wardrobe kitted out with smart, bespoke suits and casual wear. The kitchen was stocked with his favourite piroshki, small pies filled with ground beef, and an ample supply of meatballs. Perhaps, more pertinently, no expense had been spared with the drinks cabinet. His vodka and whisky of choice lined the shelves.

MI5 had done their homework well and knew how to keep their prized Soviet double agent happy. It was a nice touch all the same. Ivanov appreciated their thoughtfulness.

As Lewis continued to show them around the mews house, the easy-going banter between his MI5 minders continued unabated. However, it was patently evident to Ivanov that Joyce still remained very much in charge of the security operation.

CHAPTER 10

St Barnabas Mews
Chelsea, South West London

By the end of the week, they had fallen into something of a routine. Weather permitting, Ivanov was more often than not to be found sitting in the tiny courtyard garden, reading a raft of books in both Russian and English.

Carter would invariably volunteer to take on the night shift. Ivanov figured there was probably method in his madness, as it enabled him to enjoy a few precious hours of peace and quiet.

Communications were kept to the bare minimum. Lewis would occasionally pop across the mews to check up on things, share a coffee, and give them an update, before tootling back to his observation post. Of an evening, Joyce would usually take herself off for an hour or two. Ivanov presumed to attend briefings at MI5 HQ. But, then again, it was only a guess.

Routine aside, he still found it all but impossible to relax. At night, sleep tended to come fitfully. He'd wake up time and again, going over things in his head. However, well-meaning Joyce was, he missed Bradley's company and steadying hand.

Up until now, despite the risk of constant discovery, he'd always managed to retain a semblance of unflappability. Still, over the last few days, everything had come to a head and was beginning to take a heavy toll, not only physically but also emotionally.

The profound feeling of helplessness and loss of control over his life was immense. He desperately wanted to be able to trust Joyce, but life as a spy had left him with a somewhat jaundiced view of human nature. An air of suspicion continued to permeate his every thought and action.

Without Bradley, Joyce was his only lifeline and interface with MI5. Unlike Bradley, she was impossible to read. You never quite knew what you were going to get—the deadly volcanic temper or the charm she could turn on like a tap. Mercurial or not, Ivanov was finding it increasingly not to like her.

She'd tried hard to reassure him, but he still felt more exposed than ever and repeatedly questioned MI5's decision not to transfer him to the Fort. Joyce's response was always the same; that it was entirely out of her hands, and the mews had its advantages. Situated in a quiet cul-de-sac, there was only one means of access; from a security aspect, it was relatively easy to protect with round the clock cover.

Ivanov's eyes held Joyce's for a fraction of a second as she walked over to the television and angrily switched it off.

'I was watching *that!*' he protested.

'I couldn't hear myself speak.'

'Then you should have said something!'

'I did, but you couldn't bloody hear *me!*' Joyce pointed to the television with a sharp, stabbing motion.

Ivanov found himself mumbling a half-hearted apology. As she made to leave the room, his voice stopped her mid-stride.

'There are times you trouble me, Miss Leader.'

'Trust me; it's a two-way street!' she snorted sarcastically.

He heaved his shoulders. 'I'm just a little curious; that's all.'

She gave a weary sigh. 'Go on. You're obviously dying to say something or other, just spit it out and get it off your chest!'

'Well...for someone who would appear to have the ear of Sir Spencer Hall, I'm a little surprised that

I've never come across your name before. Unless, of course, *Leader* isn't your real name.'

A slow bemused smile worked its way steadily across her face. 'It's real enough.'

'Then I can't quite understand how you've managed to stay under the KGB's radar for so long.'

'Maybe your people aren't quite as slick as you think they are,' she threw back.

'Perhaps,' he agreed, 'but I think there's probably a good and logical reason why we haven't tracked you down.'

'I have a feeling, Alexei, that even if your people had spotted me either here or in Germany, knowing how they operate, they'd automatically assume I was some low-ranking clerk or secretary,' she said acerbically. 'You see, being a woman does sometimes have its advantages.'

Ivanov conceded she might have a point. The KGB usually employed women in fairly low-ranking roles, but more crucially as sexual bait. He guessed Spencer had likely turned his colleague's long-prescribed assumptions to MI5's advantage. However, Joyce was still the exception within the Service's ranks; post-war, very few had managed to work their way to the top.

'Tell me something,' Ivanov asked, a little awkwardly. 'Of all the people Spencer has at his disposal, why on earth did he give *you* the assignment?'

A smile resurfaced on her lips. 'I think you might be better off asking him yourself.'

'But I'd rather hear it from you.'

Joyce took a moment before answering. 'Well, believe it or not, Alexei, *we* actually have a great deal in common.'

He looked doubtful, not quite sure what she meant.

'I was a double agent during the war,' she explained, in an almost relaxed conversational tone.

Joyce always possessed the ability to surprise him, but this time, she'd completely wrong-footed him. Ivanov didn't quite know how to react. Was she merely toying with him or being deliberately provocative? He really hadn't a clue.

'A double agent,' he repeated warily. 'Who… who were you working for?'

True to form, Joyce didn't miss a beat. 'The Abwehr, the Nazi Intelligence Agency,' she said, without a shred of emotion.

A look of undisguised horror creased his face. 'I'm sorry, Miss Leader, if that's meant to be some kind of joke…'

'I assure you, it's not a joke,' she cut in sharply.

The bitterness and the atrocities of the past still ran deeply with him. Operation Barbarossa, the Axis codename for the invasion of Russia, had resulted in twenty million Soviet deaths. He'd lost both his parents during the war. After being taken prisoner, his father's SS guards had brutally executed him, and his beloved mother had eventually slowly starved to death in besieged Stalingrad.

Ivanov still couldn't entirely take it all in and began fumbling agitatedly for his Gauloises. Stuffing a cigarette between his lips, he sneered across at her. 'What in God's name was Spencer thinking of assigning, a former *Nazi* agent…' Ivanov struck a match and lit the Gauloises. 'Your accent,' he blustered. 'It's…it's perfect; I'd never have taken you for a *German*.'

'I'm Anglo-Austrian,' she corrected him. 'I was educated in England.'

'Does that make any difference?' he asked scathingly.

'Well, it does to *me*! I worked alongside Spencer during the war.'

Unimpressed, Ivanov inhaled a long draw on his Gauloises.

'In the lead up to the D-Day landings, I fed the German High Command with bogus intelligence about the Allies' plans.'

'I'm sure you did,' he said derisively.

'I did what I had to survive.'

'And after the war?'

'I joined FIAT-BIOS.'

Ivanov took another puff, thoughtfully savouring the pungent smelling French cigarette. He recalled that shortly after World War II, with the support of their Allies, the Americans had set up an organisation called the Field Intelligence Agency Technical (FIAT). The BIOS arm of the setup was the British Intelligence Objective Sub-Committee and had been located in Frankfurt.

A recommendation from Spencer would have undoubtedly carried considerable weight with the Americans. That put a whole different slant on her standing within the intelligence community. Perhaps he'd been too quick to judge.

The team she headed up, Joyce explained, was almost exclusively military officers on assignment, plus a few civilian support and secretarial staff. They were already well aware that apart from the atom bomb and radar, the Allies were lagging far behind the Germans in scientific advancement.

Their task was to investigate and pursue the Nazis "wunder" technology, and in particular, their talented rocket scientists, before the Soviets captured them—men who were now crucial to President Kennedy's expansion of the US space program.

'After FIAT and BIOS, what happened...where did you go?'

'What else could I do? I returned to London and was lucky enough to be invited to re-join the Service.' She smiled, looking at him carefully. 'A few years ago, I decided that I needed a break.'

'And?' he quizzed her.

'Spencer allowed me to take a step back.'

Ivanov shook his head and smiled sympathetically. 'Come on! In our game, *we* both know there's no such thing as retirement *or* taking a step back!'

For the first time since they'd met, her laughter seemed entirely genuine. 'I haven't been active for the last five years.'

'So, what happened?'

'You know the drill. Let's just say, it was an offer I couldn't refuse!'

He winked at her knowingly. 'It always is.'

Under normal circumstances, both her pedigree and, more crucially, gender would have denied Joyce's continued employment at the epicentre of Britain's post-war intelligence service. Even experienced female members of WWII's Special Operations Executive hadn't fared quite so well and often had, frustratingly, found themselves surplus to requirement.

Active or not, why on earth had they failed to pick up on her before now? How had she managed to slip the KGB's attention for so many years? Apart from her involvement with British Intelligence, more intriguing was her work alongside the Americans.

Maybe she'd been right all along, that the KGB possessed an inherent blindness where women were concerned. Stunningly attractive or not, Joyce had obviously still been dismissed out of hand in both London and Frankfurt as no more than a low-ranking clerk or secretary, rather than the head of the British (BIOS) office.

Ivanov wanted to dig a little deeper and discover more about her, but knew he'd be wasting his time. He ended up saying the first thing that came to mind.

'There must have been times in your life when you've faced almost certain death,' he blurted out of the blue.

Joyce stared back at him curiously.

'Were you ever afraid of dying?'

It struck her as a particularly odd question. 'You'd have to be a bloody fool not to,' she said dully, as the phone started ringing and interrupted their conversation. 'Excuse me,' Joyce apologised, picking up the call.

The flashing red light on the intercom indicated it was Lewis. 'Hi, Dave. Is everything okay?'

'No, it isn't. We've spotted two bandits,' he answered, his voice sounding strained.

'Are they on foot?'

'No, they're travelling in a blue Triumph Herald 1200.'

'Where are they now?'

'Apparently, they're circling the area.'

'I'll let Jed know,' she said curtly, ending the call.

'Is anything wrong?' Ivanov asked.

'I guess we're about to find out.'

CHAPTER 11

Pimlico Street
Chelsea, South West London

Dave Lewis's forward surveillance team was based in Pimlico Street, guarding the only entrance to St Barnabas Mews. He was also responsible for the combined MI5 and Special Branch deployment in the surrounding area.

Between them, they'd managed to pick up on a blue Triumph containing two young male occupants. A combination of experience and gut instinct told them something wasn't quite right.

The car had made a couple of short stops before finally pulling over in Pimlico Street. To the untrained eye, they appeared to be lost and were busily checking out a folding roadmap.

The lead team noted the vehicle's registration number and called through the details to MI5's Ops

Room. The response from HQ was immediate. Keep them in sight, if possible, and take a closer look at the occupants, preferably on foot.

Shortly afterward, a grey-haired woman of slight stature appeared from around the corner. Enid Burdis was an old hand, experienced, and had spent most of her working life as a respected intelligence analyst.

In her younger days, Enid had been a valued field officer and viewed the occasional distraction as a welcome relief from the humdrum routine of ploughing through endless transcripts and cables. It took a particular intellectual mind-set to be good at what she did, but deep down, she often hankered after the adrenaline fix of field work.

As instructed, Enid casually made her way along the street and passed Lewis's team without so much as a second glance, before continuing toward the Triumph. She seemed a little doddery and slightly unsteady on her feet. Every so often, she stopped to peer at one of the enticing window displays in the upmarket shops lining the street, before casually opening the catch of her handbag. Rummaging inside, she withdrew a silk handkerchief along with a small silver compact. Flipping it open, she raised it, pretending to have something in her right eye and began dabbing it with the handkerchief.

After a little adjustment, Enid decided she had an almost perfect angle of the two young men in the Triumph and swiftly depressed the button on the hidden camera inside the compact.

Satisfied she had several close-up shots, Enid slipped the compact back inside the handbag, snapped it shut, and unhurriedly retraced her steps.

Drawing level with the lead surveillance car, she mouthed silently, "Bagged it!" and moved on past.

Although the photographs would undoubtedly prove to be useful, right now, Lewis desperately needed some feedback about the Triumph's registration plate. He'd assumed they were false, so when the call finally came through from the Ops Room, he was taken aback the vehicle was, in fact, registered to the Downham Trade Institute. Was it perhaps just a little too obvious? He wasn't quite sure. Why would they be that careless, unless they wanted to be seen?

The Institute regularly organised trade missions to Britain and was currently hosting a delegation from East Germany. The Triumph was allocated to two senior engineers who had arrived a week later than the rest of their *supposed* trade colleagues. It was slightly unusual, but not entirely without precedent. As with all Eastern Bloc trade missions to the West, it was expected a proportion of the attendees would, in reality, be members of their respective intelligence services.

Either way, his surveillance team had been spot-on in singling them out so quickly.

It was only a hunch, but Lewis suspected that Vasiliev had dispatched men to sound out the location. It was a shrewd move. The two supposedly lost delegates were undoubtedly Stasi officers.

The Stasi, or State Security Service, was one of the most feared and hated institutions of the East German government. Although their power was seemingly all-pervasive, the truth was somewhat different. They were no more than puppets of their Soviet political masters.

Although the Stasi's primary role was domestic surveillance, their remit also encompassed foreign intelligence, which was mainly directed against their capitalist neighbours across the Berlin Wall in West Germany. The various trade missions provided an ideal cover for rather more covert operations.

The two men were unlikely to be little more than foot soldiers and, in Moscow's eyes, expendable. They certainly hadn't stumbled randomly upon the mews and were likely to have been on a fishing trip, not only to check out the safe house itself, but to try and establish the extent of MI5's security ring surrounding it. Besides, Lewis didn't believe in coincidence.

HQ confirmed the two engineers, along with the other delegates, were based at a hotel in Paddington. Their busy itinerary, apart from official visits arranged by the Institute, was located in and around the vicinity of their hotel.

No doubt Vasiliev wanted to keep his *own* people in reserve for the main play against Ivanov. Did they intend to kidnap him? Or, more likely, make an attempt on his life?

Beneath all the Germans' overt display and

shenanigans, Lewis figured there was a subliminal message to British Intelligence, and more especially to Vasiliev's opposite number, Sir Spencer Hall, that someone had leaked Ivanov's location to the KGB, and Moscow still retained the upper hand.

⸺+ +⸺

The phone rang again. It was Lewis; the blue Triumph was heading into the mews.

Joyce glanced over her shoulder to Carter. 'They're here.'

Carter slipped an automatic into a slender suede holster and eased on a jacket.

'Take care,' she called after him.

Joyce opened one of the sideboard drawers and retrieved her Walther PPK and checked it was loaded before moving over to the window. She gingerly peered through the net curtains to see Carter step outside the garage. The Triumph had already come to a stop at the end of the cul-de-sac. His gaze roamed from the car toward the first-floor window opposite. Lewis gave him a quick thumbs up sign to confirm they had his back if anything kicked off.

Carter's motorbike was parked in front of the black painted garage doors. He casually took his time apparently checking it over, before climbing on to start the engine and began revving it up.

The Stasi officers still hadn't moved. They appeared to be consulting a roadmap, but, even so, it was evident to Carter they'd already eyeballed him. He decided to switch off the engine, dismounted and crouched down beside the bike, and began tinkering with the engine.

Almost immediately, the Triumph began heading back down the mews toward him. Carter's pulse quickened. Apart from the gun in his holster, there was also a handgun concealed beneath the bike's seat. He braced himself, but had the feeling if they were serious, something would have kicked off by now.

As the Triumph drove on past, its two male occupants deliberately made brief eye contact with him. Once they were out of view, Carter stood up, slipped a handkerchief out of his trouser pocket, and began wiping the engine grease off his hands.

Lewis came across the mews to join him. 'Did you get a good look at them?'

'Good enough.'

'What do you reckon?'

Carter crunched the oily handkerchief tightly in his fist. 'It's pretty obvious they wanted to be seen.'

'Hmm, I wonder what the boss will make of it all.'

Carter smirked. 'If I were you, Dave, I wouldn't even try to fathom out what the old bugger thinks!'

He shrugged. 'You might be right.'

Long before the flap with the Triumph and its East German occupants, Ivanov's frustration at being cooped up at the mews was already at breaking point, but this proved to be the final straw.

Vasiliev was playing them all like a fiddle; infiltration of British Intelligence at the very highest echelons had led the Germans to the mews. In his opinion, MI5 was now nothing more than a busted flush, and he'd placed his life on the line for nothing.

Joyce didn't react to his diatribe and allowed him to vent his anger. As Ivanov continued pacing the room with his customary histrionics, she occasionally took a considered sip of a large and much needed martini. On a positive note, he was almost beginning to run out of steam, but sadly, not quickly enough.

It ran through her mind that he was just another assignment like so many others. But whether Ivanov lived or died was ultimately immaterial to her. She'd do her duty, of course, but no more than required. Would she go the extra mile to save his life? Well, right now, Joyce doubted it.

The man was too full of himself, of his own self-importance. Valuable or not to Western intelligence, in her opinion, Ivanov wasn't a particularly likable man. Then again, the feeling was probably entirely mutual.

CHAPTER 12

MI5 HQ/Ops Room
Central London

Standing with his arms folded at the rear of the Ops Room, Spencer's presence was tangible, adding to the tension.

His arrival during a live operation was rare and had immediately cranked up both the pressure and the stakes, keeping everyone on their toes. He'd slipped in unannounced, but had kept a respectful distance from Alan Kidd, the duty operational commander.

Kidd had recently been promoted into the job and, long before today's unfolding operation, had already felt under increasing pressure to prove himself.

Enid Burdis's photos of the East Germans were currently being developed in the basement lab. But knowing the Enid of old, Spencer didn't doubt for a minute her ability to have come up with something useful.

The initial plan was to run them through the Service's ID records. If they failed to come up with anything, then they'd widen the search, sharing them with Scotland Yard, Interpol, and other allied intelligence agencies. Either way, it was still a long shot and would take time, but time was the one thing they didn't have on their side.

Without high-level penetration of the Service, Vasiliev would never have been able to stay a step ahead of the game. Someone had leaked Ivanov's location. The only unknown was whether or not the leaks extended to both sides of the Atlantic.

Mirsky, the CIA's double agent, had recently paid with his life. Was the same source also responsible for Ivanov's betrayal? It remained too early to call, unless, of course, they were being played a double bluff by one of their Soviet agents.

Although the safe house in St Barnabas Mews was compromised, Spencer was also deeply conscious that any rash knee-jerk reaction might well end up playing into the KGB's hands.

Whatever happened, at some point, they would have to relocate Ivanov, but where and when? He'd need to weigh up all the options, for it wasn't only Ivanov's life on the line, but those around him.

The radio traffic between the various surveillance teams and Kidd continued reverberating across the otherwise hushed Ops Room, as Vasiliev's stooges began turning out of St Barnabas Mews. The messages came in sharp bullet points.

'Where are they heading?' Kidd said.

'Toward Sloane Street.'

Kidd glanced up at the large map pinned in front of his desk. *What the hell were they playing at?* he asked himself.

There was a slight lull.

'They've taken a right out of Sloane Square.'

'Along the King's Road?'

'Yes, sir.'

The East Germans were certainly giving their people a run for their money. If nothing else, it certainly proved they weren't dealing with a couple of genuine stray trade delegates lost in the backstreets of London. Then again, expendable or not, Vasiliev wouldn't have dreamed of dispatching a couple of middle-ranking amateurs to sound out the mews.

During another lull in the comms, Kidd stretched forward, resting his elbows on the desk. Until recently, he'd been a successful, uncompromising field man. In the past, several of his colleagues had failed to make the often-tricky transition to the Ops Room.

Kidd desperately needed to contain the situation. But the way things were starting to pan out, it seemed increasingly likely they might well end up losing the Stasi team in the heavy traffic.

Kidd picked up his large white mug, but then

realised he'd long since drained its dregs. He set it down again and began drumming his fingers impatiently on the desk top, waiting for what seemed like an eternity for the radio to crackle back into life.

Why me, and why now? Kidd thought to himself. If he screwed this one up, it was a potential career breaker. He was still only six weeks into the bloody job when Ivanov had decided to defect! Right now, a lot was riding on his decisions, especially with the boss listening in on his every action and command.

Frustrating or not, the occasional radio silence provided him with a small but welcome respite. Kidd was rapidly running out of ideas to contain the situation.

Although appreciating Spencer's decision not to intervene, right now, Kidd needed Spencer's advice. But whether he'd view it as a sign of failure or not was a moot point.

Kidd glanced over his shoulder. He caught his boss's eye. Spencer was still standing in the darkened recesses of the Ops Room.

Seeing him turn, Spencer's gaze drifted slowly over the younger man's face; it was etched with anxiety. Slowly unfolding his arms, he moved unhurriedly through the serried ranks of his staff toward the front to the Op Commander's desk.

So far, he'd been quietly impressed by Kidd's performance. It was his first significant combined intelligence and Special Branch operation. He had handled the situation, at least outwardly, calmly and professionally. Given the additional pressure of having MI5's Director General watch his every move and utterance, it was no mean feat.

On reaching Kidd's desk, the radio comms crackled back into life. The Triumph was reported to be heading south past Chelsea Barracks toward Battersea Bridge.

All eyes in the Ops Room were now firmly fixed on the boss.

'Is there anything I can do to help out, Alan?' he asked, his velvety tones filling the intermittent void between the communications.

Kidd signalled to his deputy, Viv Matea, and temporarily flicked over control. 'With due respect, sir, I have a feeling that things are probably starting to get just a little *above* my pay scale,' he admitted readily.

Spencer appreciated his frankness. Given the top-heavy priority surrounding Ivanov's security, there certainly wasn't any shame attached to his asking for help and, in effect, handing over command of the op.

'I take it you've called in every available team?'

'Yes, sir.'

'Then I don't know about you, Alan, but I think it's high time we stop playing cat and mouse with our East German *friends*...at least for today, don't you?' His calm, authoritative voice cut through the tense atmosphere like a knife through butter.

The radio traffic continued apace in the

background, as Matea carefully tried to keep track of the situation.

'I think it's probably high-time we crank things up a little and start to reel the buggers in.'

Kidd held his eyes expectantly.

Spencer inclined his head toward the array of telephones banked on Kidd's desk and pointed to the green one. It was the direct link to the Special Branch Ops Room based at Scotland Yard.

'Ask for a uniformed patrol car to pull them over.'

A flicker of hesitation crossed Kidd's face.

'I wouldn't worry yourself. Garvan's people usually find an excuse. Dangerous driving, or whatever they fancy. Trust me, Alan, they'll come up with something. They always do.'

Kidd began scribbling on his notepad.

'Make sure their Ops Commander knows *we* need to have them taken off the road immediately and pulled in for questioning at the nearest available nick.'

'Yes, sir, but he might want to get the okay from...'

'The Assistant Commissioner?'

Kidd nodded.

'I'll square everything off with Garvan. In the meantime, just get things moving.' He made to leave, but as an afterthought, added, 'If you run into any problems with the Yard, just mention my name. Tell them the Director-General has personally ordered the car is to be taken out.' He shot him a wry smile.

'From what I understand, it usually makes quite a difference.'

'Yes, sir,'

'Give me a call when they have them in custody.'

Kidd was on the point of responding, but Spencer was already on his way out of the Ops Room.

CHAPTER 13

St Barnabas Mews
Chelsea, South West London

'Alpha is approaching. Repeat, Alpha is approaching.'

It was Spencer's codename.

'Do you have visual?' Lewis asked.

'Confirm, sir, we have visual.'

Lewis handed the receiver over to a colleague and moved over to the window in time to see a black taxi turn into the mews and park up outside Ivanov's safe house. A grey Ford Zephyr was close on their tail and drew in behind the cab.

British Intelligence owned a small fleet of cabs. They provided an unobtrusive way of travelling across the capital, without as much as a second glance. Well, perhaps only from the occasional irate punter who would offer up a stream of abuse as one of their faux taxis sailed past without stopping. But, all in all, it was a relatively small price to pay for the anonymity the cabs provided.

Spencer waited inside the taxi until given the all-clear to move. It was only then that Joyce emerged from the garage to meet him.

'I'm sorry we're running late, but we got caught up in a traffic jam along Victoria Embankment,' he apologised.

'Had anything happened?'

'Emergency roadworks. The Gas Board had dug up half the bloody road to fix a leak.'

Stepping inside the garage, Joyce thanked him for coming at such short notice.

He produced a long, low, rumbling chuckle. 'Is Comrade Ivanov still kicking up rough?'

Joyce rolled her eyes.

'It's not like you, Jo, to call in the cavalry.'

She scrunched up her face. 'I always knew it wasn't going to be an easy ride, that things might be a little difficult, but…'

Spencer looked at her questioningly. 'But what?'

Professional or not, his constant mood swings and occasional melodramatic outbursts had almost reached a breaking point with her.

Joyce took a deep intake of breath. 'I figured it was either call you in or finish the bastard off here and now!' she admitted.

His brows furrowed, a scowl forming. 'Surely, to God, things can't be that bad, Jo?'

Her expression said it all. 'After the Stasi stuff kicked-off, things have gone from bad to worse.'

Spencer smiled slightly. 'I guess he's probably running scared, Jo.'

'Who wouldn't be, but if he carries on like this...'

'Bastard or not, we need to keep the bugger alive, at least for the time being,' he said, making his way up the spiral staircase.

Joyce stared up at him. *What the hell was that supposed to mean? He was up to something, but what?*

'Have you heard anything from Garvan lately?' Spencer called down, without looking back.

Gripping hold of the metal bannister, she stared up at him. 'No, why should I?'

On reaching the landing, Spencer waited a beat and made to say something, but Joyce was already in full swing. As straight-talking as ever, she demanded to know whether Garvan had asked him to say something about her calling an end to their relationship.

'No, he hasn't,' Spencer said bluntly.

'Really?' she quizzed sarcastically.

'It's the truth,' he assured her.

For once, Joyce felt inclined to believe him. 'It wasn't working,' she explained in a rush. 'I had to let go...to move on.'

Spencer paused for a second, before adding measuredly, 'Well, you've certainly taken the wind out of his sails.'

'Has he told you why I called off the wedding?'

'I can't say as he has. He was pretty cut up about it all, that I do know.'

Joyce smiled a slight bitter smile; her nostrils flared as if enforcing her derision. 'Luke couldn't understand my decision to re-join the Service.'

'You never actually left... No-one ever does.'

'Then *you* try telling him that.'

'Oh, come on, Jo, he knows more than most people how things work with *us*. Your file was simply on hold. You wanted a break from the Active List; I signed it off.' Spencer shrugged indifferently.

'Perhaps Luke believed I was the exception to the rule.'

Spencer suspected her willingness to return had probably been the perfect excuse to escape the prospect of married life with Garvan and the yawning humdrum of leafy suburbia. At the time of her request to leave, Joyce was craving peace. She'd needed to do something else in an attempt to regain some semblance of normality, where her life wasn't always on the line, and no longer revolved around the demands of the Service.

But, as the months passed, Joyce had grown tired of so-called normality. As much as she desperately wanted to step away from the Intelligence world, after a while, she had found herself increasingly bored. By her own admission, Joyce began to miss the day-to-day adrenaline rush and the close camaraderie.

Although life outside MI5 was initially appealing, over time, it had increasingly begun to pall. Spencer's decision to bring her back into the fold eventually came as something of a welcome relief. Albeit, it was a decision that had unwittingly caused the eventual breakdown of her relationship with Garvan.

To his surprise, an unexpected smile swam across Joyce's face. 'If you must know, for some reason or another, the stupid sod's convinced himself I only agreed to return because of *you.*'

Spencer stared back at her blankly. '*Me*? What the hell's got into him?'

'He's convinced himself I'm in love you.'

Spencer exploded with mirth. 'Oh, for Christ's sake, Jo, now I know he's lost the ruddy plot!'

Now that it was said and out in the open, as she expected, Spencer had made light of it and continued up the stairs chuntering under his breath.

'Why did I know you'd say that,' she whispered to herself.

⋙+ +⋘

Ivanov was stretched out on the sofa, listening to their muffled voices emanating from the staircase. Although the living room door was partially ajar, their voices remained too indistinct to catch any meaningful conversation. Hearing Joyce's uninhibited laughter precede their way into the living room. Ivanov noted her voice seemed lighter, more relaxed than he'd heard before. Perhaps Spencer had made some joke or other.

Ivanov found himself glancing expectantly to the door as it was pushed wide open. Smiling broadly, Spencer reached out to shake his hand, greeting him warmly.

For all his uneasiness, Ivanov was slightly disarmed by his unexpected sincerity. Spencer breezily apologised for the recent incident with the Stasi at the mews. He seemed entirely genuine, but then again, it was difficult to tell, although he certainly appeared to be in an unusually mellow mood, which was disconcerting in itself.

With the East German trade delegation's visit to the UK currently attracting positive press inches, Spencer explained glibly that Her Majesty's government was somewhat reluctant to create an unnecessary diplomatic incident. In exchange for dropping a range of "trumped-up" traffic violations, it had been quietly agreed with the East German authorities that the bogus delegates were to be dispatched on the next available flight back home.

Perhaps it was no more than Ivanov had expected, and he accepted the decision with quiet resignation. The outcome was a classic case of diplomatic posturing, a strategic game where everyone saved face. Still, the subliminal message remained all the same: that the Stasi officers had been caught red-handed.

To his surprise, the charm offensive continued unabated. Spencer was full of questions and concerns. Were his people taking good care of him? He was engaging and engaged. At times, self-deprecating, but remained throughout as sly as a fox and sharp as a tack.

He looked to Joyce and airily gestured toward Ivanov. 'I see Alexei's glass is empty.'

Her face remained devoid of expression, as she followed his gaze toward the empty glass. Ivanov had been steadily hitting the bottle since mid-morning. She'd tried her best to keep him relatively sober until Spencer's arrival. From now on in, she figured it wasn't her problem.

Without comment, she scooped up the cut crystal glass off the coffee table and headed over to the drinks cabinet. 'I take it you'll be wanting something yourself as well?'

The mirthful look in Spencer's eyes said it all.

'Your usual?' she queried flatly.

'No, I really rather fancy a bourbon. Do we have any?'

Joyce inspected the cabinet. 'Jack Daniels?'

He gave her a thumbs up.

'On the rocks?'

'Yes, thank you.'

'How much longer am I to be stuck here?' Ivanov interrupted tetchily.

'I'm not sure, Alexei. But not too long. I just have to square a few things off with Assistant Commissioner Garvan before we make a move.'

Ivanov inclined his head, giving a sharp little grunt in response.

Even on a good day, Ivanov could be somewhat chippy, and today certainly wasn't a particularly good day.

Forcing a slight smile, Spencer wearily eased himself into an armchair. He pulled a pack of Players cigarettes from his pocket and set them aside. 'Tell me something, Alexei, does the name Stephan Egorov mean anything to you?'

Ivanov racked his brains for a moment before shaking his head. '*Nyet*, no, I can't say as it does.'

'Hmm, interesting,' Spencer pondered.

'Should I have done?'

'I'm really not sure.'

'Who is he?'

'Egorov or, should I say, Major Egorov, is a former *Spetsnaz* officer.'

As Joyce handed out their drinks, he repeated uneasily, '*Spetsnaz*?'

'Yes. We've managed to ID him from the surveillance photos taken outside the Embassy's compound. He was seen talking to one of your shadows.'

'Have you identified the others?'

'Yes, we have. Egorov was already on our radar, so it was relatively easy to confirm. The others have taken a little more time to track down.'

'Are they *Spetsnaz*?' Ivanov asked with a catch in his voice.

'Yes, …they're all ex-special forces colleagues of Egorov. They also have something else in common.'

Ivanov looked strained and leaned forward, cupping his glass in both hands.

'In January, the four of them were transferred, lock, stock, and barrel, onto the KGB's payroll.'

'So they're Dima Vasiliev's chosen men.'

'Well, that's one way of looking at it.'

Ivanov chose his words carefully and kept his temper in check. 'Don't play with me, Sir Spencer. My life's on the line here!'

Spencer took a slow sip of the Jack Daniels, explaining their Intelligence sources had indicated that long before Egorov's formal transfer to the security service, he had already participated in several key KGB operations for Vasiliev.

They assumed it was paramount for the London team to be led by an officer who couldn't only assume command and total loyalty from his men. But if things went wrong, he was acutely aware of the possible far-reaching consequences of their actions on the ground.

He believed the squad's equipment, including a large stash of ammunition, had probably been smuggled into London via the Soviet Embassy prior to their arrival.

'Did they enter the UK separately?'

Spencer didn't want to commit himself and brushed over it. 'We've tracked them down to an apartment reserved for junior clerks and ancillary staff.'

'In Goodge Street?'

'Yes.'

Employing former members of the *Spetsnaz* placed an entirely different, and somewhat, deadlier slant on things. They would be Vasiliev's men to the core, and out with the usual rank and file of the KGB. While Ivanov accepted there were sound and logical reasons why Vasiliev had sent unknown faces to London, why would he have called on the services of former special forces soldiers when he could have deployed any number of experienced in-house KGB officers? But, maybe, it was more about bringing fresh blood to the organisation in an attempt to consolidate his power base.

'So they killed him!'

'Bradley?'

'Yes. But why would Vasiliev have wanted him liquidated? There was no need to.'

'Perhaps he was on to something.'

Ivanov held his gaze for a fraction. 'Who knows… perhaps he was.'

Spencer didn't comment.

'What do your CIA cousins make of it all?'

'I'm not sure.'

'Have they found a link?'

Spencer knitted his brows. 'I'm sorry, what sort of link?'

It was an effort to keep the irritation off his face. Ivanov didn't quite succeed. 'You're playing games with me, Sir Spencer.'

'Am I?' he answered, placing a cigarette between his lips.

Ivanov snorted derisively. 'I think we've both been around long enough to realise there's no such thing as coincidence, at least not in *our* line of business!'

His comment elicited a slight smile.

'It's staring you in the face.'

'Is it?' came the non-committal answer.

'Then try placing yourself in my shoes for once, Sir Spencer, how would you feel? Can't you see the nets closing in?'

Spencer flicked on his lighter. 'You mean Anatoly Mirsky?'

'Yes,' Ivanov snapped. 'His body's barely cold. He was the CIA top agent…someone outed him, and he ended up paying with his life. So, is it merely a coincidence that a few weeks down the line, they're also onto me?'

'What are you suggesting?'

'I doubt if I need to spell it out to you.'

Spencer rolled the cigarette carefully between his thumb and forefinger. 'Infiltration on both sides of Atlantic?'

Ivanov nodded. 'Yes, high-level access.'

'If you're right, Alexei, it's still going to take time to root them out,' he said, taking a puff on the cigarette.

Ivanov raised his hands in agreement.

'I think we both agree Mirsky was good at what he did, but I always felt he was never quite in your league.'

Ivanov felt faintly flattered, although he suspected Spencer was about to follow-up with some killer punchline. He'd almost have been disappointed if he hadn't.

'The trouble is, Alexei, if you're right about a top-ranking mole operating out of the UK, from where I'm sitting, I can't help wondering why, as the KGB's No.2 in London, you didn't pass on their name to us?' Spencer leaned forward, stubbing out his half-smoked cigarette. 'Unless, of course, you've deliberately been kept out of the loop.'

Ivanov smiled to himself, at least he'd been right about the punch line, but it wasn't quite the one he'd been expecting. But by default, he was understandably on the backfoot.

'I swear to God…' he tried protesting.

'What's God got to do with it?' Spencer cut across him irritably.

'Isn't it obvious?'

'I only wish it was, Alexei.'

'Can't you see there's a pattern? Whoever they are, they have to be in Vasiliev's back pocket.'

'I've no doubt they are, which begs another question. He apparently trusted you enough to give the go-ahead for your posting to London, so why would he hold out on you?'

'After Paris, I was the obvious choice. Besides, it was probably easier to run with it, rather than kick up a fuss.'

'Even so, Vasiliev could still have overruled your appointment.'

'On paper, yes, of course, he could have.'

'So, what stopped him?'

'I hadn't put a foot wrong in France. I'd made a number of usual contacts, fool or not, Vasiliev knows where to draw the line. The old guard, the Politburo, the people that *really* matter, supported my transfer to London. Given a free hand, I wouldn't be sitting here!'

'Are you saying that's why he kept you out of the loop?'

'I've no idea,' Ivanov countered tersely.

'But Vasiliev would have needed help here on the ground. It'd be practically impossible to run a top agent sitting in Moscow Central without having someone here on the ground in London to handle them.'

Ivanov agreed with him.

Spencer's smile was cold. 'Presumably, someone perhaps like your boss, Comrade Smolin.'

'Yes,' he replied bleakly.

'I still can't quite decide if we've simply miscalculated your importance, or whether you've been playing us along like a fiddle.'

Ivanov threw his hands up in despair before angrily slamming his glass down, spilling its contents across the table.

'I've risked everything spying for the British Intelligence...even the safety of my family!' he shouted, his eyes suddenly burning with tears. 'I can do no more, Sir Spencer. In all but name, I'm a dead man walking. I'll spend the rest of my days looking over my shoulder, wondering and waiting for the KGB to catch up. Trust me...they'll find a way. They always do!'

CHAPTER 14

St Barnabas Mews
Chelsea, South West London

Joyce checked the Walther PPK was fully loaded and ready to go before carefully opening the door. Ivanov was lying on his back, fast asleep, snoring loudly in fits and starts. Light flooded in from the hallway into the darkened bedroom. It was six-thirty in the morning.

Not wishing to startle him, Joyce quietly approached the bed and gently brushed the back of his hands. Ivanov stirred slightly at her touch.

'Alexei,' she whispered, once again sweeping her fingertips across his hand.

He snorted fitfully and wearily opened his eyes, blinking at the unexpected intrusion of light.

'Alexei,' she said, her voice soft, yet urgent.

Still, half-asleep Ivanov yawned and propped

himself up on the pillows. 'What's going on?' he blustered irritably.

'We have to move.'

'*Move?*' he repeated tiredly.

'You need to get yourself dressed.'

Bleary-eyed, his gaze traced her across the room. 'Why, what's happened?'

Joyce stopped; her figure silhouetted against the glare of light from the hallway and made a show of looking at her watch. 'You've ten minutes to get yourself ready,' she said sharply.

Ivanov was still struggling to wake up. 'Where are we going?'

'Just get yourself ready, Alexei. You'll find out soon enough,' she said, closing the door on him.

Taking a moment or two to gather himself, Ivanov wiped the sleep from his eyes, before swinging his legs over the side of the bed. He then padded barefoot across the bedroom and pulled back the heavy brocade curtains to let in the early morning light.

Opening the wardrobe, Ivanov reached for a small leather suitcase and began scrambling around inside, throwing in a change of clothes. After a quick wash, he gathered up his shaving kit and a few spare essential toiletries. Closing the suitcase, he was good to go with a minute to spare.

Still damp from an overnight downpour of heavy rain, sunlight glistened on the cobbled mews. Carter was already waiting for them beside a large, racing green Rover 105 with a supercharged engine. MI5's version of the popular car was an altogether different beast from the conventional production line models.

Carter loaded Ivanov's suitcase into the boot and opened the rear door, allowing Ivanov to ease himself onto the backseat. 'There's a pillow and blanket on the back shelf,' he said.

Ivanov peered over his shoulder. 'Thank you,' he answered, reaching for them.

'Make yourself comfortable, but whatever you do, keep your head down and out of sight.'

Somewhat reluctantly, Ivanov did as he was ordered and curled up in a foetal position, making himself as comfortable as possible, before Carter helped cover him over with the blanket.

Joyce opened the driver's door and placed a handbag on the floor behind the seat. She then leaned across to double-check the Rover's console; it was stashed with an ample supply of ammunition before getting in behind the wheel.

Having retrieved the roadmap from the boot, Carter jumped in beside her.

'Are we ready?' he asked.

'As ready as I'll ever be.' She smiled.

Starting up the Rover's powerful, throaty engine, Joyce quickly glanced back to reassure herself Ivanov was still curled up and covered over by the blanket. It crossed her mind; he really couldn't have been too comfortable, but it was either that or place him in the boot, which she knew wouldn't have gone down too well with her irascible Soviet charge.

'Are you okay back there?'

Ivanov merely grunted in response. 'Where the hell are we going?' he demanded.

'To the Southwater Estate in West Sussex.'

'I've never heard of it.'

'There's no reason why you should have.'

'It's just south of Horsham,' she explained.

Ivanov was still none the wiser. As the Soviet's "supposed" Trade Secretary, his position had automatically afforded him diplomatic status. Although he'd made a point of visiting most of the leading city's outside of the capital, beyond the major urban conurbations, his geography of the UK was somewhat sketchy.

On his arrival at the Embassy, he'd been shown a classified KGB document, listing several properties owned by British Intelligence dotted around the country, many of them with rural locations, but not exclusively. At the time, it'd been just another strand of intelligence, but it certainly hadn't been his highest priority.

Joyce drove off slowly along the mews, coming to a halt at the end of the road. Carter leaned forward slightly and pointed to a sleek black Jaguar heading along Pimlico Street toward them, with its headlights flashing. Lewis was behind the wheel accompanied by one of his team.

Joyce raised her hand in acknowledgement before taking a left and falling in behind the Jag. Following them out of the mews was another backup car, driven by a member of Garvan's close protection officers, Lew Lillywhite.

CHAPTER 15

Transfer to Southwater Estate
Horsham, West Sussex

Radio communication between the three cars and the Ops Room was kept deliberately tight. Scrunched up on the backseat, Ivanov closed his eyes, listening out for the slightest sound. Be it a change of gear or the screeching brakes of another car, intermingled with the muffled voices of people on the streets. At every junction and set of traffic lights, Ivanov's already high pulse rate lurched in anticipation as the Rover's engine dawdled over. There was always more chance of an attack when they were stationary.

The convoy travelled south over the Thames and then along Kennington Road, where they joined the A24 at Clapham. The busy road still followed the same route as the old Roman road of Stane Street, which continued heading steadily south out of the capital.

Other than risking running the odd red-light, Joyce had managed to keep pretty close behind Lewis's lead vehicle. They'd only been forced to separate on two occasions, at a busy roundabout and then at a congested T-Junction, but it was no more than they had expected.

The further they drove from central London and out toward the leafy suburbs of Merton and Sutton, the constant, relentless thrum of the city slowly began to fade.

Ivanov started relaxing slightly and asked their permission to sit up, complaining that he'd developed a severe cramp in his left leg and was twisting and turning in pain on the slippery leather backseat.

Carter looked across at him. 'Just stay where you are.'

Ivanov threw back the blanket. 'I need to move my leg!

'I'm sorry, Alexei. You've gotta keep your head down.'

Ivanov swore under his breath, but apparently not quietly enough.

'And the same to *you*, my friend,' Carter responded in fluent Russian.

Begrudgingly, Ivanov pulled the blanket back over himself.

'How much further do we have to go?' Joyce queried.

Unfolding the roadmap slightly, Carter studied

their route. 'We should start seeing signs for Dorking shortly.'

Joyce instinctively glanced in her wing mirror. Lillywhite was still reassuringly right on their tail. 'So, once we hit Dorking, how many miles is it to Horsham?'

Carter carefully traced his finger across the map scale. 'I'd say a little under thirteen miles. It's certainly no more than that.'

⚌╬ ╬⚌

After having successfully negotiated their way through the attractive market town of Dorking, the convoy quickly crossed the county border from Surrey into West Sussex. They eventually turned off the A24 at Kingsfold, a small village, and continued through a place called Roundthorpe, yet another picturesque village dominated by a large thatched inn and an impressive church spire. From there, they soon found themselves in the meandering lanes and roads crisscrossing the Sussex countryside. The only traffic they encountered was the occasional car or agricultural tractor, trailing produce from one of the many local farms.

After a further two miles, the convoy reached a fork in the road. Joyce stuck to Lewis lead like glue and slowed up behind him, before turning into a narrow hedge-lined lane.

'God, this is a bit tight, isn't it!' Joyce cursed. 'Do you think Lewis knows where he's going?'

Carter shrugged, re-checking the map. 'I'm sure he does.'

'Well, let's hope so!'

Although the sunlight filtering through the dense canopy of trees was beginning to wane behind the increasing cloud, the almost constant flashing through the leafy branches was still blinding. Joyce squinted, screwed up her face, and hurriedly slipped on a pair of stylish Oliver Goldsmith sunglasses to shield her eyes.

Slipping them over the bridge of her nose, she caught a sudden movement in the wing mirror, accompanied by the sound of a motorbike at full throttle closing in on them fast. The noise was deafening, and the speed at which they were approaching came as a shock.

'Jed,' she said coolly, 'have you...'

'Got it,' he answered, withdrawing a pistol.

The bike rider and his pillion seated behind him were kitted out identically with helmets and goggles.

'What do you reckon?' Carter queried.

'I'm not sure, but I guess there's only one way to find out.'

On the back seat, Ivanov felt a sudden cold knot of fear in his stomach. 'For Christ's sake, what's going on?' he begged them.

Carter re-checked the pistol's chamber was fully loaded. 'There's a motorbike on our tail. Just cling on tight, Alexei. Things might get a little uncomfortable.'

Ivanov let out another Russian expletive.

Seeing Joyce flash the Rover's headlights, Lewis immediately floored the accelerator down hard. With the risk of a possible attack, they needed to keep moving and avoid stopping at all costs; if they did, it might well end up proving to be fatal.

As the convoy speeded up, the motorbike continued to keep pace and started to ease alongside Lillywhite's car. Hurtling through the narrow lanes, Lewis only hoped to God they didn't encounter any oncoming traffic. Otherwise, they'd all be screwed.

In a bid to block the motorbike from passing them, Joyce swung the Rover to the right-hand side of the lane. It was a standard blocking movement, the three cars now racing nose to tail, with hopefully little, if any, chance of their being overtaken.

Twisting round in his seat, Carter saw the pillion rider produce a grenade from his leather jacket and pull the pin. He released the leaver and lobbed it toward the Rover.

Carter was on the point of saying something, but it was obvious Joyce had already seen him. Hearing the grenade bounce on the roof, they both instinctively ducked down and braced themselves for the inevitable explosion.

The grenade spun off and arched off into the undergrowth before exploding in a blinding flash of white light, followed by an ear-splitting crack. The aftershock drove the air out of their lungs as shards of splintered trees, hedgerows, and a myriad of stones and other debris blasted into the passenger side of the Rover. Joyce and Carter briefly exchanged glances, realising that only a combination of sheer luck and speed had saved them from almost certain death.

The explosion ripped Lewis's rear metal bumper clean off, sending it hurtling off into a nearby field. Lillywhite's car suffered a similar fate, destroying not only its bumper, but also its front headlights were blasted clean out.

Apart from a few dents and cracks, the convoy's bullet-proof glass and armour plating had luckily withstood the explosion. However, if the pillion rider lobbed another grenade, they might not be so lucky.

Although he'd been unable to prevent the attack on the convoy, Lillywhite knew he needed to react quickly. Seeing the guy reach into his jacket for another grenade, he slammed hard on his brakes and deliberately smashed into the motorbike.

The momentum somersaulted both riders into the air, before crashing back down on the road. Their powerful bike careered off into a tree before finally coming to rest in a cornfield. A brief smile of satisfaction crossed Lillywhite's face before suddenly losing control of the car. It struck the righthand side of the lane and then swerved to the left in a bid to regain control before colliding head-on into a tree. The front end completely caved in, and smoke started rising from the engine.

It had all happened so fast, almost in slow motion. It crossed Joyce's mind that it'd be little short of a miracle if Lillywhite had survived the crash.

Lewis came through on the comms. 'Do we stop?' he asked anxiously.

'No, we keep moving,' she ordered. 'Call in a Red Alert to HQ. Rear escort disabled, two bandits down.'

CHAPTER 16

HMS Dolphin
Royal Navy Submarine School
Hampshire, England

Apart from the base commander, Captain Tony Beatty, and Rear Admiral Turner from the War Office, who had accompanied Spencer on the trip from London, no-one else at *Dolphin* knew they were playing host to MI5's Director-General.

The duty rumour circulating the naval base was that their "civilian VIP visitor" was probably some important scientific boffin from the Ministry. Whoever he was, Beatty had certainly pulled out all the stops to ensure their visit ran as smoothly as possible.

A prototype two-man mini-submarine designed to drop acoustic microphones at strategic points along the Baltic seabed was currently undergoing sea trials at the base.

They were intended to eavesdrop on the so-called "*Kompleks*", the Soviet's 14th Submarine Squadron. The mini-sub had already undergone extensive development and was on the point of finally going live. The prospect of tapping into Soviet submarine communications wasn't only intriguing; it also offered a potentially invaluable source of continuous high-grade intelligence.

The visit to *HMS Dolphin* had been a long-standing diary commitment for him. However, given Bradley's murder and Ivanov's subsequent defection, Spencer had seriously considered pulling out altogether. He would have done so, had it not been for the intervention of his opposite number in MI6—Sir Richard Cavendish, or Dick, as he was known—urging him to take a good look around the place. It was important stuff, and he'd appreciate Spencer's thoughts about the project.

In some ways, it was an offer he'd almost felt unable to refuse. The respective sister organisations were historically stove-piped in their rather different approaches to intelligence gathering, but also riven by a past of deeply entrenched internal rivalries and mutual distrust.

Dick Cavendish had been brought out of retirement to head up the, at times beleaguered, MI6. Its members were still reeling from several high-profile spy scandals. Within the political and intelligence community, Cavendish was viewed as a safe pair of hands, someone who could guide MI6 through what had been a particularly turbulent period and help bring the organisation back onto an even keel. Since being appointed, things had improved and moved on immeasurably. Morale had increased, and he appeared to be sorting things out.

Although the sister departments had invariably experienced a somewhat fractured relationship, Cavendish viewed the divisions and ongoing internecine war as not only divisive, but potentially damaging to the overall effectiveness of British Intelligence. From day one, he'd made it his mantra to mend the bridges between them.

While Spencer had accepted the need to forge closer ties, it was still unfortunately set against a raw backdrop of deep-rooted mistrust. Less than a year ago, George Blake had been outed as the latest in a long line of MI6 officers convicted of spying for the Soviet Union.

Spencer was of the firm belief his MI6 colleagues, including Cavendish, had been blindsided, motivated by some arcane misguided loyalty in *their* refusal to believe that any of their people could be capable of ...in their words, such "ungentlemanly" conduct. In Spencer's experience, they worked to a different set of rules. Trust was hard-won. Differences aside, Cavendish had remained a friend of longstanding.

Whatever Spencer's private thoughts about past failings, he had respected the decision. Cavendish had been brought back on board to root out a seemingly endemic corruption within the ranks of MI6 and to get a firm grip on the foreign arm of British Intelligence. On a personal level, he had always enjoyed Cavendish's company and was impressed by his often-astute observations.

Spencer realised the invitation to *Dolphin* was an olive branch and a small but significant step toward reconciliation.

Despite his initial reluctance to visit the base, much to his surprise, Spencer had actually ended up thoroughly enjoying Captain Beatty's guided tour of the establishment, more especially his chats with the young submariners tasked with operating the mini-subs. He was on the point of eagerly climbing into one of the prototypes, when Freddy Evans, his driver, entered the secure facility escorted by a heavily built Royal Navy policeman or, as they were officially called, Regulating Petty Officers.

A look of surprise crossed Captain Beatty's face. His guards were under strict orders not to interrupt the VIP visit. 'Tyler, what the hell...'

Evans cut Beatty dead mid-sentence. He accepted responsibility and apologised profusely for the intrusion, before addressing Spencer. 'I'm sorry, sir, but you need to call the Office immediately!'

'Yes, of course,' he said, turning to Beatty and requested to use a secure phone.

'If you'd like to follow me, sir, you can use the one in my office,' he said, leading the way.

Spencer fell in beside Evans, asking him quietly, 'What the hell's going on, Freddy?'

'We've had a call on the Jags comms from HQ, sir; there's a flap on, a Red Alert.'

They stepped outside the rather dreary, grey-bricked blockhouse housing the mini-subs into a knife-keen wind and a fine drizzle of rain sweeping in from the Solent, the strait of sea separating the mainland from the Isle of Wight. Spencer pulled up the collar of his jacket and followed Beatty across the vast open square to another equally dreary looking block housing the Captain's office.

Spencer thanked him and waited until Beatty had closed the door before picking up the secure red coloured telephone and dialling the Op Commander's direct line. There were a few prolonged clicks before Alan Kidd eventually picked up the call.

'DG here. I understand you contacted Evans about a Red Alert?'

'Yes, sir, I did,' he said, immediately recognising his voice.

'What's happened?'

'There's been an attack on the convoy.'

Spencer paused slightly. 'Do *we* have anyone down?'

'Lew Lillywhite.'

'Just Lillywhite?' he asked carefully.

'Affirmative.'

'And the opposition?'

'Two. A motorbike and pillion rider...both down.'

'Is everyone else safe?'

'Yes, sir.'

Kidd quickly briefed him about the attack. Raising a Red Alert automatically set in motion a well-exercised response from MI5 and Special Branch. The scene of the incident, Kidd explained, was still in the process of being cordoned off and secured. The contingency plan had been activated, providing additional support teams on the ground, who were already on their way to the safe house near Horsham.

'Have you spoken to Assistant Commissioner Garvan about the incident?'

'Not personally, sir, only with his Ops Commander.'

'Okay, that's fine.' Spencer thanked him, adding tersely, 'But I'd like you to place a call to the Yard on *my* authority and tell them I need a priority ID on the motorbike riders.'

CHAPTER 17

Southwater Estate
Horsham, West Sussex

After the attack, the remaining battered convoy drove on for another two miles before turning onto the Worthing Road. They cut through the tiny village of Southwater with its sprawling brickworks, and were joined outside a pub by local police tasked with escorting them on the final leg of their journey.

Beyond the outreaches of the village, they arrived at the high-stone walled perimeter surrounding the Southwater estate. Although the property still belonged to the Charman family, the house and grounds were requisitioned during World War II. Through various subsequent lucrative arrangements with the Charmans, the estate continued to remain in government hands and, in particular, to British Intelligence.

Following Lewis through the impressive gated entrance, flanked by castellated stone pillars, Joyce dropped the Rover into second gear before driving over the metal cattle grid set into the road.

'What's going on?' Ivanov groaned in pain.

'Don't worry. We've made it to the safe house,' she assured him.

'May I sit up now?'

'Yes, you can.'

Ivanov thanked her, wincing he tried easing himself up on the backseat. During the attack, he'd crashed heavily into the well of the car and suspected he might have broken a couple of ribs. He was certainly finding it difficult to breathe.

Having cleared the cattle grid, they were stopped by two plain-clothed Special Branch officers carrying automatic weapons. They checked Lewis's vehicle out and then moved toward the battered Rover. Joyce opened the window as one of the officer's crouched down beside them, his eyes swiftly taking in each of them in turn, before settling his attention once more on Carter.

'It's good to see you again, Jed!'

'And you too, Will!'

Although they'd spoken recently over the phone, it had been a while since they had actually worked together.

'It must be what, all of a year ago?' Carter beamed.

'And the rest. I think you'll find it's probably nearer two.'

Joyce slowly lowered her sunglasses off the bridge of her nose and peered over the top at the tall, well-built police officer.

'Miss Leader, isn't it?'

'Yes, it is,' she said, squinting, slipping the sunglasses back up again.

During their conversation, Carter had mentioned in passing his boss was attractive, but his description certainly hadn't done her justice. *You lucky bastard!* Will couldn't help thinking to himself.

'I'm surprised you managed to make it in one piece,' Will said, taking in the damage to their car.

'I suppose we were,' Joyce answered crisply. 'Do you have a medic on standby?'

'We have an army nurse.'

'And a doctor?'

'A retired colonel. He lives locally in Horsham.'

'Can you patch a call through to say that we need our *guest* checked over? He might have broken a rib.'

He glanced at the back seat; Ivanov was hunched over, clutching his side.

'Yes, of course, ma'am. I'll see to it right away.'

Joyce thanked him. 'I take it there hasn't been any sign of trouble?'

'Yes, not a whisper. Everything's secured and locked down.'

'Good, then I take it we can start heading off to the house.'

While her smile remained pleasant enough, Will realised she was understandably anxious to move off. He inclined his head and stepped away from the car and waved them on.

Driving off behind Lewis, Joyce rewound the window before passing Carter a sideways glance. 'What did you say his name was?'

'Will...Will McDowell'

'So, where do you know him from?'

'We met on a surveillance job in Mayfair.'

'No, I guessed that much. He's got Special Branch written all over him. Is he any good?'

'You've no worries there, Jo. He's got ten years under his belt with Garvan's mob.'

She nodded without comment.

Carter looked back at Ivanov, who was still in obvious discomfort. 'We'll get you sorted soon enough.'

'Thank you,' he whispered.

The long tree-lined driveway cut a straight swathe through the rolling open parkland. In the distance loomed a classical Georgian mansion with a shimmering, circular lake stretched out to the foreground.

'Her Majesty's government certainly can't be short of a few quid to keep this place going,' Joyce observed dryly.

'Not bad, is it.' Carter smiled, peering across the lake. 'Lewis tells me he knows the place quite well.'

Joyce glanced across at him questioningly.

'Apparently, he's been here a few times with our lord and master.'

'With Spencer?' she queried.

'Yes.'

'I don't quite know Lewis's full history, do you?'

Carter shook his head. 'I haven't a clue, other than that he's an ex-naval engineer. To be perfectly honest with you, Jo, I've never actually liked to ask him. Then again, I'm not entirely sure whether I'd get a straight answer.'

'You're probably right,' she agreed. 'I'd just like to know why they're as thick as thieves, that's all. There's gotta be a reason, but what is it?'

Carter rolled his eyes and laughed. 'God, that's a bit rich, isn't it, coming from you?'

'I wouldn't know, you tell *me*?'

'The whole of bloody department knows you and the boss are just the same!'

'Maybe.' Joyce smiled slightly, killing the conversation dead.

Lewis led the way. Sweeping past the mansion, they drove through a rather grand porticoed entrance into a courtyard styled stable block, which now served as garaging for government vehicles.

Drawing up alongside him, Joyce switched off the engine and, puffing out her cheeks, allowed herself a sigh of relief. She took a moment, gathering her thoughts, realising Lillywhite was unlikely to have survived the crash, but without his quick thinking and selfless actions, Joyce knew they wouldn't have escaped with their lives.

Although in considerable pain, Ivanov shuffled

forward slightly to pat Joyce's shoulder. 'Thank you,' he whispered.

It was a kind gesture, and one she certainly hadn't expected. She smiled and looked back at him in acknowledgment. Surprisingly, it meant a great deal to her.

CHAPTER 18

The Southwater Estate
West Sussex

Shortly after arriving at the estate, Joyce received a call from Alan Kidd at MI5's HQ, who confirmed Lew Lillywhite had died at the scene, along with the two motorbike riders. Joyce whispered her thanks to Kidd, before thoughtfully replacing the receiver. His death wasn't unexpected, but it hit her all the same. She knew Lillywhite was married with two young children. The eldest, a girl, had only recently started school, and her little brother was barely six months old.

With tears shimmering in her eyes, Joyce moved to the window overlooking the lake. Lillywhite's bravery had cost his family dearly…too dearly. Hurriedly wiping away her tears, Joyce needed to compose herself before breaking the news to the others. She simply couldn't afford to break down, especially not in front of Ivanov.

The attack only served to enforce their greatest fears: that someone at the very highest level of the Service wasn't only out of control, but continuing to leak like a sieve to Moscow Central, and perhaps more crucially, with a direct link to the head of the KGB.

It was still difficult getting her head around the idea that it was possibly someone she knew, and perhaps someone she'd worked alongside and trusted.

Joyce gathered them together in the spacious drawing room lined from floor to ceiling with linenfold panelling salvaged from a local Jacobean mansion, which had fallen into disrepair shortly after the war.

Ivanov looked strained as he shuffled awkwardly across the room, complaining his painkillers hadn't kicked in. Although still in considerable pain, the duty doctor reassured him that he was thankfully suffering from nothing more serious than torn muscles.

'Give it a little more time, Alexei. If they're not working, we can always ask the doctor to up the dosage,' Lewis said in his customary, quiet, thoughtful voice.

'Maybe you're right,' he winced, perching himself uneasily on the cushioned window seat.

'You certainly don't look okay,' Carter observed, settling into a plush sofa.

'It's worse since I moved,' Ivanov puffed.

After his examination by the nurse, he'd been propped up in bed, but Joyce had insisted he join them downstairs.

Closing the heavy oak door behind them, Joyce apologised curtly to Ivanov for asking him to come downstairs and thanked him. But had thought it necessary. In truth, she'd felt unable to repeat the news of Lillywhite's death without breaking down.

Holding his side, Ivanov stared across the room at her expectantly.

There was no really easy way of breaking the news; steeling herself, Joyce relayed Kidd's message practically verbatim. It somehow seemed a little easier that way.

Carter and Lewis were visibly upset on hearing of Lillywhite's death, as was Ivanov in his own, taciturn way.

So far, his decision to defect had cost the lives of two young men. First Bradley, and now a police officer, whom he'd never personally met, but who had, without doubt, saved all their lives at the expense of his own.

An awkward, slightly uncomfortable silence filled the large drawing-room. Each alone with their thoughts, until Ivanov felt compelled to break it. He needed to voice his feelings that until the traitor was taken down, there'd probably be an even greater loss of life.

To Joyce's mind, it wasn't so much what Ivanov had to say; it was more to do with his annoying, fractious delivery, almost to the point of being condescending. She'd had enough and rounded on him. Seeing the rage on her face, Ivanov realised it was one thing to voice his concerns, but quite another to sound so ungrateful, especially just a few hours after Lillywhite had lost his life in defending him.

'For Christ's sake!' she exploded. 'I think we've all worked that one out for ourselves, and until we discover who's behind the leaks, then I guess we're both in the same ruddy boat!'

Ivanov arched his brows questioningly.

'Up shit creek without an effing paddle between us!'

Carter had once described Joyce as possessing the eyes of Caligula and the beauty of Lucretia Borgia. At the time, Ivanov had dismissed it as nothing more than a back-handed compliment, albeit one delivered with genuine admiration and affection. Likewise, Lewis had frequently referred to her occasional blow-ups akin to witnessing a hairdryer on full blast.

There'd always been a certain antipathy between them. Perhaps understandably, it had now all come to a head. He'd always known she was tough and uncompromising; however, he had never experienced a full-frontal explosion before.

Out of the corner of his eye, Ivanov caught the bemused exchange between the two MI5 officers. It was only now that Ivanov began to realise the two men had been far from joking with him.

Having vented her anger, Joyce headed for the door. Unprofessional or not, she'd needed to put him back in his box.

Reluctantly, she turned to face him, her expression still filled with contempt. 'The coroner has agreed to release Bradley's body.'

'When?'

'In the morning.'

'And the funeral?'

'I'm not sure.'

'Will the Prime Minister be there?'

'Trust me, he'll milk it for all it's worth,' she said acerbically.

Ivanov expressed his surprise. He didn't quite know what she was getting at; they'd been good friends.

'Well, only up to a point. Friendship aside, the PM has only one agenda; *survival*. It boils down to column inches in the press. Behind all those public appearances on the steps of No.10, expressing his grief, Prime Minister Hawley,' she said witheringly, 'is more concerned about some bright spark journalist raking up a connection between you and Bradley.'

'And what if they do?'

'They'll slap their editor with a D-Notice.'

The government rarely issued D-Notices and

then only as a supposedly advisory note to the media that reporting be discontinued for reasons of national security. Given Bradley's closeness to the PM, there'd be a great sucking of teeth in Fleet Street, but as yet, they hadn't broken ranks.

CHAPTER 19

MI5 HQ
Mayfair, London

Spencer's secretary, Dawn Abrams, nudged open the door carrying a stack of files when the telephone started to ring. In a rush to take the call, she stumbled, lost her grip, sending them crashing, spewing classified documents across the dark brown linoleum floor.

'Oh, for f...k sake!' Dawn cursed in frustration, before grabbing hold of the receiver before the caller hung up. 'DG's office,' she answered sharply.

'It's the switchboard here, Miss Abrams. You have a caller on the line from Langley HQ.'

'Thank you.'

Calls from the CIA's headquarters were usually pre-arranged to ensure Spencer was in office to receive them. There was certainly nothing scheduled in the diary, unless, of course, something urgent had come up unexpectedly.

Manoeuvring her way around the desk, Dawn plonked herself down on the swivel chair. 'Who is it, anyway?'

'It's Mr. Stein,' the telephonist answered.

'Okay, put him through.'

Jack Stein was a close friend and ex-war colleague of Spencer's and had recently been promoted as the Deputy Director of the CIA.

Dawn had a great deal of time for the ruggedly good-looking Stein. Within security circles, he was affectionately known as the *silver fox*. He was certainly universally popular with MI5's female staff, and word of his arrival in the building invariably spread like wildfire. Secretaries and clerks alike usually found some tenuous pretext or other to visit Dawn's office, in the hope of "accidentally" bumping into the CIA's charming Deputy Director. In fact, it'd become something of a running joke between her female colleagues.

She glanced across at the office clock. Langley was five hours behind UK time. In the States, it was still only early morning. Whatever it was, had to be important.

Waiting for the call to be patched through, Dawn's gaze flickered toward the files spread out across the floor. It'd take ages to cross-reference the documents and piece them all together again.

The telephonist came back online. 'I have Mr. Stein for you, Miss Abrams.'

'Thank you.'

'Dawn, are you there, can you hear me, how are you?' he asked.

Recognising his familiar, laid-back drawl, she couldn't help smiling to herself. 'Yes…yes, I can, I'm okay, how about you?'

'I'm doing just fine. Thanks for asking,' he said cheerily, before adding as an afterthought, 'Well… apart from the fact I'm still figuring out how to play the grown-up.' He only half-joked, referring to his recent promotion.

Dawn laughed. 'Yes, I bet you are!'

Stein came with a reputation of shooting from the hip and speaking his mind with few, if any, filters. Perhaps unsurprisingly, being the CIA's Deputy Director, his limited patience and diplomacy were often stretched to breaking point.

For once, the transatlantic connection between London and Langley, Virginia, was crystal clear. Over the last six weeks, they'd experienced an increasing number of technical issues with their respective secure lines. Most of the glitches had proved to be relatively minor. However, a few remained unexplained, leading to an increasing suspicion the KGB had deliberately targeted them in a concerted effort to infiltrate the system.

'I just wanted to tell you that I'm flying over to London,' Stein continued chattily.

Dawn glanced down at her diary. She knew he wasn't due to come over until the end of the month to attend a conference.

'I was wondering if there's any chance of us doing lunch while I'm in town?'

'Well, I'll think about it, Jack,' she answered coolly.

'Great,' he said, before asking if he could have a quick word with Spencer.

'Yes, you're in luck, Jack. He's just got back to the office. Hold on a sec, and I'll patch you through.'

———

After a pause, Jack heard Spencer say with genuine affection, 'Jack, you, old *bastard*, what's this all about? Dawn mentioned something about your flying over tomorrow?'

'Something's come up…it's hot off the press.'

'I don't suppose it's anything to do with our mutual friend, is it?'

'Yeah, well, you could say that.' Stein paused slightly. 'Have you managed to ID either of the motor cycle riders?'

'We know for sure one of them was Stephan Egorov.'

Stein pursed his lips and let out a long silent whistle. Egorov was quite a scalp, and it must have taken a whole weight off Spencer's mind.

'And the other one?' he asked reflectively.

'We're almost certain it's Andrei Bobrik. His face was a bit battered up after the accident, so it's taking us longer than we'd like to identify him.'

While the *Spetsnaz* team might well be severely depleted, Egorov's second-in-command, Peter Galin, was still out there, and came with a ruthless reputation, as did Sergey Yudin, the fourth member of their beleaguered hit squad. Either way, they continued to pose a severe threat to Ivanov's safety.

'Listen, Spence; we *need* to talk.'

There was a moment of hesitation down the line. 'It's down to you, Jack. If it's that important, I'll clear my diary, just give me a time.'

Stein slunk back in his chair and calculated by the time he touched down at London Airport and was picked up, then driven to his hotel in Westminster; he'd need time to freshen up a little, so guessed it'd probably be a good four hours after his arrival.

'If it's okay by you, shall we say about six o'clock?' Stein suggested.

'Where do you want to meet up...at your hotel?'

'No. I reckon it might be better if I swing by yours.'

Spencer scribbled a note on his inkpad. 'You take care now and have a safe flight.'

'Thanks!'

CHAPTER 20

London Airport

J ack Stein emerged through Customs; his sunglasses hooked casually in his top breast pocket. He was met in the arrivals hall by a junior member of the CIA's Embassy staff.

On recognising him, Stein reached out to shake his hand. 'Paul Blum, isn't it?'

'Yes…sir,' he stammered, surprised, if not a little flattered, Stein had remembered his name.

They'd met fleetingly at an Embassy reception back in January. Stein made it his business never to forget a face or name and always made a point of ensuring junior members of the CIA and Embassy staff alike felt at ease in his company. In Blum's opinion, Stein's relaxed, seemingly easy-going manner only served to underpin his authority.

'Can I take your suitcase for you, sir?' Blum offered.

Stein thanked him, passing it over. He retained a tight grip on a leather attaché case, containing top-secret documents, handcuffed around his left wrist. The cuff was discreet and neatly disguised beneath the sleeve of his suit.

Greetings over, they began threading their way through the crowded arrivals hall.

Outside the main terminal building, a diplomatic plated black Cadillac was waiting to whisk Stein off to the St Philip's Hotel in central London. Blum opened the rear door for him, before quickly placing the suitcase into the boot of the limousine.

Stein settled back and acquainted himself with the smart, dark-suited driver in his crisp white shirt and polka dot tie. Wayne Hunt possessed a slow Texan drawl and was apparently on his first posting outside of the States. On first impressions, he struck Stein as being a little on the serious side. He couldn't quite decide whether Hunt was merely nervous, or it was just his way. Whatever it was, Hunt certainly wasn't the talkative type.

Shortly after they left the airport, the heavens suddenly opened. Driven by a strong wind, sheets of rain bounced off the pavements, sending rivulets of water gushing along the gutters. As the drains struggled to cope with the heavy deluge, the Cadillac smoothly swished through a spray of increasingly large puddles.

Stein gazed distractedly at the passing traffic, barely noticing the droplets of rain streaking across the passenger window. He began fiddling with the handcuff and flexing his fingers. It seemed a little tight after the long flight.

Given his seniority as Deputy Director, he really hadn't expected to find himself as little more than a glorified courier. Initially, they'd toyed with the idea of sending the intelligence via an encrypted signal. But both the White House and his boss, Chas Brennan, the CIA's Director, had come to a consensus that the contents were so explosive, they should be delivered by hand, and in particular by *Stein*.

It had briefly crossed his mind that maybe he should have warned Spencer off in advance. But in the end, Stein had decided to err on the side of caution. Besides, he didn't have official permission to give his old friend a heads up.

There were justifiable fears and suspicions on both sides of the Atlantic concerning how widespread the KGB had penetrated their respective organisations.

The attaché case contained a smoking gun, confirming that neither side was entirely watertight or immune from Soviet penetration. The material was so sensitive, only the President and his closest staff were aware of its contents. They'd finally managed to track down the mole behind Ivanov's betrayal. Their source was an old hand, deeply embedded within the Politburo itself. However, a recent elevation to the all-powerful Central Committee had not only broadened their brief, but by default, had supplied the CIA with their codename; *Wolf.*

Admittedly, it wasn't much to go on, but at least it was a start. After countless hours of sifting through endless heaps of intercepted intelligence and transcripts, and then re-checking with all their sources, they began to realise they were on the right track, and the net had finally closed. But Wolf's identity had only opened up a Pandora's Box.

The news had ricocheted around Washington's elite political inner circle like wildfire, coupled with a sense of almost disbelief. It simply couldn't be right; surely, there must be some kind of mistake.

Before going live, President Kennedy had ordered the CIA to double-check their raw intelligence. Wolf's identity was politically explosive. Kennedy needed reassurance; they couldn't afford to screw up.

Within an hour, Chas Brennan, the CIA's Director, had confirmed nothing had changed and happily signed off his report to the President.

Even so, for the White House, it was still a difficult call, but having weighed up the risks, Kennedy, albeit reluctantly, had agreed to keep the lines of communication open with British Intelligence, at least for the time being.

If Spencer Hall was as sound as Brennan and Stein assured him, then the President would be willing to share America's intelligence on Agent Wolf. It was their call, but God help them if they were wrong.

After their somewhat terse meeting in the Oval Office, Stein had found himself as the appointed courier of the grim news.

Wearily slipping a Chesterfield cigarette between his lips, Stein patted his pockets. 'Do either of you guys have a light?' he asked.

'Yes, sir,' Blum answered.

'Thanks,' Stein said, reaching forward for the lighter.

It was his first in over ten hours. Although in his mind he was on a mission to pack them in altogether, Stein couldn't help enjoying the occasional nicotine fix, and right now, he desperately needed one.

'I don't suppose if either of you knows whether I've been booked into Room 201?' he asked, handing Blum's lighter.

'Yes, sir, I checked before we left the Embassy.'

Stein offered up an appreciative smile. Blum had obviously done his homework, for there were very few things in life that truly bothered him. He certainly wasn't usually given to over-sentimentality, but ever since the war, 201 had continued to be his hotel room of choice.

During World War II, the St Philip's Hotel had been a long-standing haunt the UK's various intelligence agencies. In the latter stages of the war, the hotel had also enjoyed the enthusiastic patronage of America's covert Office of Strategic

Services or the OSS as it was more commonly known during the war, before developing into the modern-day Central Intelligence Agency (CIA). Such was their love of the place; it had almost become a semi-official annex for them. Since 1945, fortunately, nothing much had changed, and it was still a quiet oasis in the heart of London.

The grand Victorian building was shaped like a sprawling horseshoe around a pretty courtyard garden lined with trees. The grand foyer and grand double staircase, for Stein, possessed a certain welcoming theatricality.

Such was Stein's attachment to the place that the US Embassy annually block-booked his favourite room cum suite. He wasn't usually particularly picky. There were few places, other than the St Philip's, where he felt entirely at home, and although other high-profile visitors to the UK enjoyed its palatial comforts, the CIA's Deputy Director, without fail, always had the first claim.

CHAPTER 21

MI5 HQ
Mayfair, London

Spencer's office was all Chippendale furniture and plush red carpets. He had inherited the décor from his predecessor. It wasn't particularly to his liking, but he simply couldn't be bothered to have it redecorated. On rare occasions, junior officers were invited to the inner sanctum. The majority of the chosen few had penned some report, which had garnered his interest. Behind his back, they often jokingly referred to him as the "illustrious presence".

Stein stood with his back against a large sash window, hands thrust deep into his trouser pockets.

Spencer was at his desk, taking the occasional sip of tea as he carefully digested the contents of the CIA's explosive report, line-by-line. His expression steadily darkening with each page. The report

171

wasn't just a smoking gun; it could quite potentially destroy any last vestige of trust between Washington and London.

'I can always come back later, if you like?' Stein suggested.

Spencer glanced up at him. 'If it's all the same to you, Jack, I'd much rather you stayed on.'

He shrugged. 'I'm happy either way.'

'Would you like another coffee?'

'No thanks, I'm fine.' Stein smiled, tweaking the net curtain to continue watching an argument between an irate driver and a traffic warden, who'd just slapped a fine on his windscreen.

Stein's shared wartime experience with Spencer had left an abiding, almost sacrosanct understanding and friendship between them. Few of their colleagues quite understood their deep-rooted closeness and bond of loyalty to one another.

After World War II, they had both been forced to adapt to what they often considered to be a somewhat tedious, post-war grind. Separately, they had adopted similar approaches to their future career paths. At heart, both men were driven and had ruthlessly worked their way through the ranks of their respective intelligence organisations. Each, in turn, had eventually garnered not only the respect of their peers, but also untrammelled influence across the broader intelligence community, including Moscow Central.

Although things had naturally moved on since the war, in essence, they both agreed, the political realities had remained pretty much the same. They'd merely ended up swapping one menacing threat for the now ever constant threat of nuclear war between East and West.

Behind them, there was a younger, ambitious generation snapping at their heels. Maybe it was just an age thing, but they often found themselves slightly out of kilter with them. Nor, in turn, could they quite get why Spencer and Stein invariably viewed the world of politics with an almost cynical, jaundiced detachment. God forbid, but perhaps it'd take another global war for them to understand exactly how they felt truly.

Spencer puffed out his cheeks and scribbled one final note on the last page of the report before angrily flinging his pen across the desk. Hearing him, Stein spun away from the window.

'I take it your source is completely kosher?' he asked, already knowing the answer, but did it all the same.

'What do you think?'

Spencer puffed out his cheeks, studying Stein's expression. 'I thought I might as well ask,' he grunted, wearily opening the bottom right-hand drawer of the desk.

With something approaching despair, he produced an unopened bottle of 25-year-old Macallan's malt whisky. Holding it aloft, he explained it was a Christmas present from Winthrop Alder, the American ambassador.

Stein's face crumpled in surprise. While Alder had many sound qualities, generosity wasn't one of them, and he was universally renowned for being tight-fisted.

'I've never received so much as a Christmas card. You've gotta be doing something right!' Stein smirked.

Spencer smiled in response. 'Let's just say; I've been saving it for a rainy day…but I wasn't quite expecting a total bloody washout!' He unscrewed the top. 'Do you fancy a wee dram?' he asked, affecting a broad Glaswegian accent.

'Sure, why not.'

Spencer pushed back his chair, grabbed a couple of glass tumblers off the sideboard, and poured two generous tots in each.

Handing him his drink, Stein asked how he wanted to play things.

'God knows, Jack!' he confessed, slumping back into his chair.

Spencer took a mouthful of the Macallan's and closed the report, staring down almost unseeingly at the CIA's crested cover. He took a sharp intake of breath before reluctantly steeling himself to focus on its title.

Wolf: KGB Codename
Identity: Sir Richard Cavendish
Position: Chief of MI6

That was just it. He still couldn't quite believe it, let alone know how he was going to handle things. Right now, Spencer readily admitted, he'd simply no idea.

He supposed there was almost a warped irony that Cavendish of all people had been outed as a KGB double agent. He'd only recently been brought out of retirement to take over the helm of the foreign arm of the Service, which was still reeling from George Blake's trial at the Old Bailey. Having been found guilty on three counts of spying for the Soviet Union, Blake had been sentenced to forty-two years imprisonment. It was a long stretch, but represented one year for each of the agents who had reputedly lost their lives through his betrayal. It was a figure Spencer still felt probably fell far short of the actual death toll.

The year before he had retired from MI6, Cavendish had found himself posted on what he considered to be a sabbatical to the CIA's HQ in Langley, Virginia, to study their current methods, protocols, and ways of improving their respective intelligence sharing.

Perhaps even more, sobering was the undoubted damage Cavendish had caused throughout his lengthy, high-profile career. Blake and his fellow traitors, Maclean and Burgess, were little short of minnows in comparison to someone of Cavendish's stature on both sides of the Pond.

In all fairness, the government had acted in good faith by deciding to bring Cavendish back into the fold. In no small part, Spencer also felt more than a degree of responsibility for his former colleague's re-appointment to the Service. Both the Home Office and No.10 had sought his advice. At the time, Cavendish was the obvious choice. The government needed someone with both the gravitas and professional integrity to control a department suffering from the seemingly continuous fall out after years of uncertainty and deep penetration by the Soviets. Spencer hadn't only willingly endorsed his candidature; his support had sealed the government's decision to the appointment.

Reluctantly, Spencer accepted Cavendish had played a blinder. But what he couldn't understand is why, after successfully duping the system undetected for decades, Cavendish had agreed to step back up to the plate. After Blake's trial, was he not just a little concerned his luck might, too, run out?

Or maybe the prospect of taking over MI6 was just a little too tempting to turn down. After all, it was the ultimate accolade and an opportunity his Soviet puppet master, Vasiliev, would never have allowed him to turn down. Whether he was reluctant or not to be dragged out of retirement, at some point, Moscow would have turned the screw and piled pressure on him to accept the government's offer.

Looking back, Spencer had genuinely believed Cavendish was getting to grips with the untold damage caused by the notorious cabal of Soviet double agents operating at the heart of MI6. The department's initial reports indicated real progress, but in hindsight, Spencer couldn't help wondering whether Cavendish had doctored or skewed the truth with the reports emanating from MI6. Whatever the facts of the matter, on both sides of the Atlantic, he'd certainly managed to pull the wool over their eyes.

With justification, the report endorsed America's fears that Britain's entire intelligence service was broken-backed.

Spencer suspected the KGB viewed the Service with contempt. Cavendish was an unexpected bonus and merely the icing on the cake. Either way, it was still a bitter pill to swallow.

Having read the report, he knew the next few weeks and months wouldn't only be critical but would take every ounce of his skill to handle the labyrinthine corridors in Westminster, while at the same time desperately trying to salvage and restore a semblance of faith in Britain's intelligence operations and its political intent.

Although Spencer feared other rotten apples were operating under the radar, Dick Cavendish was the very last person he'd have suspected capable of betraying the Service, and more importantly, his country. For Cavendish hadn't only compromised national security; in the process, he'd potentially not only jeopardised Britain's entire cross-Atlantic relationship with the CIA, but also with America itself.

Breaking the silence between them. Stein pressed him again on how he wanted to handle things.

'Well, given a free hand, I'd take *the bastard* out!'

A slow bemused smile crossed Stein's face. 'Yeah, well, back in the war, we might just have gotten away with it. But sadly, things have changed, my friend.'

Spencer raised his hand in a throwaway gesture. 'Can I keep a copy of the report?'

'Yeah, of course, you can.'

'That's good of you, Jack.' He shot him a wintry smile. 'I guess I owe you on this one. Things can't have been easy Stateside getting permission to release this stuff.'

Stein raised his shoulders dismissively. 'It wasn't just down to me,' came the laconic reply.

Spencer's brows knitted questioningly.

'The boss came on side with me. To persuade the President to give the okay to release the report, but *for your eyes only.*'

Spencer didn't know the CIA's Director, Chas Brennan, that well and suspected Stein's input had eventually won the day. 'I suppose there's only one saving grace.'

Stein narrowed his eyes curiously. 'And what would that be?'

'At least Cavendish wasn't responsible for betraying your guy, Mirsky.'

'No, but it would have been a helluva lot easier if he had,' Stein said savouring the Macallan's. 'I suppose right from the beginning, we both feared there might be two agents operating here and back home.'

Spencer began thumbing through the report; for easy reference, he'd dog-eared a number of pages. 'I can't say I recognise your mole's name. Should I have?'

'You mean Chuck Faulkner?

'Yes.'

'Sadly, our guy, Mirsky, was doomed from the moment Faulkner became his handler.' Stein paused a second before saying slowly, 'After Faulkner leaked Mirsky was working for the CIA, the writing was on the wall. It was only a matter of when and where the KGB would make their move.'

Spencer glanced up from the report. 'So, why did Vasiliev bide his time taking him down?'

Stein shrugged his shoulders. 'Standard rulebook stuff. Leave your target in place, but only just long enough to check out whether they're working alongside someone else.'

'And did he?'

'You've read the report, you tell me. Do we ever really know for sure?'

'So, what happened?'

'Things eventually came to a head when Faulkner realised Mirsky was onto Vasiliev's Swiss bank accounts...we're talking millions syphoned off. That's when he blew the whistle; he needed him silenced.'

'Where was he raking it all from?'

'Younameit—blackmail,extortion,racketeering— it's a pretty mixed bag. Vasiliev couldn't run the risk of his wheeler-dealing becoming an open secret, and certainly not in the Kremlin.' Stein drained his glass. 'After Mirsky's execution in Moscow, it really didn't take too long for us to home in on Faulkner. His fingerprints were all over Mirsky's death.'

'Do you know how long he'd been working for them?'

'We're not entirely sure; he was probably recruited back in the early fifties during his time in West Germany.

'Where was he based, Berlin?'

'No, he was posted to the CIA's HQ in Frankfurt. Back then, he was operating under an assumed name…Harry Elvin.'

Spencer recalled occasionally visiting the intelligence headquarters based in the vast IG Farben building, which was only half-jokingly known as "the Pentagon of Europe". The place had a dark, gruesome history, steeped at the heart of the Nazi regime. During the war, it had served as a deadly chemical plant producing Zyklon B – the gas used to murder countless millions of Jews and other "undesirables". Knowing its history, Spencer had always found it a rather odd, slightly disturbing experience. The building retained an almost eerie atmosphere that somehow still couldn't quite shake off its macabre past. So, Lord knows what it was like working there, day in, day out.

Stein explained that shortly after Mirsky's arrest, facing certain death, he had decided on taking a massive risk by handing his young, and hopefully impressionable, prison guard an expensive wristwatch, plus his wedding ring and a scribbled note on a scrap of paper.

From all the CIA could gather, he asked him to deliver the note to the Troika, a popular bar near the GUM store, just off Red Square. Perhaps greed had won out, but either way, the young man was good to his word. That evening he had duly delivered the seemingly innocuous note to the Troika, to Katya, the rather formidable lady, who owned the bar. Mirsky's gamble had apparently paid off.

Fearing a trap, she'd initially refused to take it. Katya was an old hand, but there was something about the nervous young man which rang true. He looked faintly embarrassed, almost like a rabbit trapped in the headlights of a car. Whoever he was, the youngster appeared to be way out of his depth. His approach was just random enough for her to suspect it wasn't an act. His voice and the bewilderment in his eyes combined to convince her; finally, this rather handsome, naïve young man was entirely genuine.

Katya held back a moment, before deciding to take a punt and offer him a drink. She pointed to a stool at the end of the bar.

As Katya continued to hold court with her customers, one of her barmen handed him a sizeable neat vodka.

After finishing his drink, she'd told him it was on the house. He'd looked slightly alarmed until the old guy beside him joked Katya only ever handed out free drinks if she fancied her customers.

Katya had then apparently winked across the bar at him. 'Are you married?' she asked the guard.

'Yes…yes, I am.'

She sighed dramatically. 'Why is it all the best ones are taken? Unless, of course, you'd like a few more free drinks?'

'Perhaps another time,' he'd stammered.

'Come here,' she'd said, drawing him across the bar to kiss him and whispering, 'Leave your note in the ashtray.'

The note had contained only two words: "Prop, Compromised."

To Katya, they were seemingly meaningless, but only three people had authorised access to Prop messages from Mirsky. His handler, Faulkner, the CIA's Director, and Stein.

It was getting just a little too close for comfort. While the British had their own problems with Cavendish, they were also facing a similar dilemma. Everyone was looking over their shoulders. The only upside was that they'd narrowed down the leak to just four agents. At the time, it didn't help any, but it was a starting point.

There was an internal investigation. Stein's loyalty had never been questioned before, but suddenly finding himself under the spotlight wasn't only distressing, it was coupled with an increasing sense of outrage.

Fortunately, for Stein and Brennan, the investigation rapidly began homing in on Faulkner's past. Ploughing back through the files, it seemed that during his stint in Frankfurt, there'd been one or two suspected leaks, never anything too serious, and in the end, Langley had apparently seen the rumours off as little more than paranoia amongst the team.

'I can understand why they might have thought that way, yeah, sure I do. But do I buy it?' Stein shrugged. 'In hindsight, there was enough evidence to take the investigation a step further. The trouble is, Faulkner's the kind of guy who's somehow always managed to come up smelling of roses...usually by passing the buck. Brennan's known him for years and really rated his work. Don't get me wrong. On paper, Faulkner appeared to have everything going for him.'

Spencer cast him a sympathetic look. 'As did Cavendish!'

'But, by all accounts, Faulkner ended up developing a bit of a gambling problem in Germany.'

'Does he still have one?'

'If he has, he's hidden his tracks well. We're still working on it.'

'Was his gambling the KGB's hook?'

Stein wrinkled his nose. 'Yes, it was. Faulkner's certainly admitted to running up sizeable debts in

Germany. He's always been on the brash side, just a little too full of himself. Come to think of it, he still is! It seems young Faulkner wasn't particularly discreet, and the Soviets made their move to recruit him. In exchange for a pile of money and an offer to clear his debts, he eventually ended up spying for the KGB. Small stuff at first, but then over the years, it spiralled out of control, ending with Mirsky's execution in Moscow!'

'Is Faulkner under arrest?'

'Technically, no, he isn't. Officially he's been suspended from duties, pending further investigation.'

'At least he seems to be talking?'

'Faulkner's been around the agency long enough to know the score. It's either talk, or we throw away the key,' Stein said, polishing off his drink. 'Which, I guess, probably brings us back to square one.'

Spencer stared at him, questioningly.

'How are you gonna handle things with Cavendish? It's your call, my friend.'

'Well, only up to a point, Jack. I'm sure I'd have heard from the PM by now if President Kennedy had called No.10.'

'Kennedy's gonna hold back until you've had the chance to brief the Prime Minister.'

Spencer thanked him. 'But I'll need to show him something,' he pondered, drumming his fingers on the report.

Stein scooped up his attaché case off the floor

and perched it on the corner of Spencer's desk. He reached inside and handed over a sealed envelope addressed for the Prime Minister's "Personal Attention". Stein explained the document had been heavily redacted. The identities of their sources and the CIA officers involved in the investigation had been removed for security reasons.

It was standard practice for both the CIA and British Intelligence to routinely redact the names of embedded agents and officers involved in current operations. Even the heads of friendly security services were rarely provided with full copies of reports.

Out with the security fraternity, the political leaders of allied governments were rarely, if ever, granted unrestricted access without prior liaison between their respective intelligence community.

Spencer placed the CIA crested envelope on a pile of paperwork in his out-tray.

'There's just one other thing,' Stein said, almost as an afterthought.

'Only the *one!*' Spencer smiled back.

'It's just that there's been a hell of a lot of speculation at Langley recently about Ivanov's wife.'

Spencer wasn't exactly surprised, but decided to play dumb and asked why.

'After his arrest at the airport, Mirsky's wife was evicted straightaway from their home, and yet, here we are, weeks down the line after Ivanov defected, and Tasha is still holed up at their Moscow flat.'

Stein regarded him carefully. 'You've gotta ask yourself why they're allowing her to stay on. The block is restricted for senior KGB officers and their families.'

'I've thought about it, of course, I have.'

'Then maybe, Ivanov isn't quite all he seems.'

'Or maybe they want us to doubt him.'

Stein wouldn't be drawn.

'Listen, Jack, I get what you're saying, but I've never taken Comrade Ivanov at face value. Do I trust him? The way things are heading, I can't even trust MI6, let alone a double agent!'

Spencer's acerbic comment elicited a crooked smile. 'If Ivanov's as good as we always believed, then why the hell didn't he finger Cavendish for us?'

'I've no idea, Jack! Perhaps we've all been screwed by him, or for whatever reason, Vasiliev decided to keep him out of the loop altogether. There's certainly no love lost between them!'

'Yeah, I suppose so,' Stein said, noncommittally.

Seeing the look of doubt cross his face, Spencer suggested it was far too early to make a call about Ivanov. They could speculate all they liked, but without hard facts, he figured his Russian spy's fate could wait for another day until they had concrete proof either way.

'You could be right,' came the slow, non-committal response.

Spencer decided to change tack and try to lighten

things by asking how long Stein intended staying on in London.

'I thought I might hang around until the end of the week...you know, just long enough to see how things pan out.'

'Good. So, we've got time to catch-up.'

'Yeah, of course, we have.'

'Any plans?'

'You mean besides taking Dawn out for lunch?'

Spencer's expression wasn't quite disapproving, but was near enough. 'I always thought Dawn had better taste in men!'

'Whatever,' Stein laughed, heading toward the door. 'Give me a call sometime.'

'I take it you're staying at...?'

'Room 201,' he said, grabbing hold of the handle. 'You take care now, and make sure you send *my* love to Joyce.'

Spencer raised his hand, a faint smile etching across his face as Stein closed the office door on him.

Finishing off the last dregs of the Macallan's, he sat a while before reaching across the desk to press the intercom. Dawn answered.

'Is Jack still with you?'

'No, sir, he said that he was running late for dinner with the American ambassador.'

'Good. I need to have a courier deliver a CIA report to No.10 right away.'

'Yes, sir.'

'And while you're at it, I'd like you to pull some files from Central Registry.'

Pen in hand, Dawn grabbed hold of her notepad and waited.

'I need everything we hold on Sir Richard Cavendish.'

There was a protracted silence on the line. 'Sir Richard?' she repeated in disbelief.

'Yes. You'd better make it a priority, and while you're at it, check out what we have on an American called Chuck Faulkner.'

'Is he CIA?'

'Yes, he apparently worked out of Frankfurt in the fifties for a while under the name of Harry Elvin. You'd better have the Registry cross-reference the records in case we hold two separate files on him.'

Dawn hurriedly made a note of the American's details on her inkpad.

'I need a meeting with the Prime Minister first thing tomorrow.'

Dawn glanced across at her diary. 'I think you'll find, sir, he's due to attend Bradley's funeral at 10.30.'

'Then fix something up for the afternoon,' he said, ending the call.

Dawn opened her desk drawer, rifled through it, and pulled out a file requisition slip, and scribbled down Cavendish, Elvin, and Faulkner's names in alphabetical order and signed it off, before heading downstairs to the registry. She was actually quite looking forward to seeing the reaction on Ian Reade, the Chief Clerk's face, when she presented the request with Cavendish's name heading the list.

By pulling Cavendish's files from Central Registry, Spencer wanted to double-check the extensive CIA report against their own personal and security files. He didn't doubt the veracity of the American intelligence, but ever cautious, Spencer wanted to read through every available shred of information the Service held on his MI6 counterpart before making a formal move against his still powerful, and well-respected colleague.

CHAPTER 22

Green Park
Westminster, London

S pencer's chauffeur-driven car pulled over on the south side of Green Park and came to a stop outside an ornate gilded set of gates. The impressive Canada Gate was flanked either side by two massive Portland stone pillars and crowned with gas lanterns mirroring the design of those surrounding Buckingham Palace on the opposite side of the road. Two bodyguards emerged from the backup car and followed Spencer into the park at a discreet distance.

The early morning sunshine had long since faded behind an increasingly leaden sky, leaving a sharp chill in the air as a brisk easterly wind whipped across the park.

Buttoning up his raincoat, Spencer headed

across the peaceful triangle of open space, populated by mature trees and undulating grassland. The park offered Londoners a quiet oasis from the surrounding hubbub of city life. Spencer always felt the park was at its very best during springtime when it sprang to life, awash with swathes of daffodils.

Spencer shot back his shirt cuff to check his watch. There were still a few minutes to spare before his rendezvous with Sir Richard Cavendish. He took himself over to a wooden park bench, withdrew a newspaper from under his arm, casually unfolded it, and began reading the front page.

Beyond the northern perimeter lay Piccadilly and nearby Hyde Park. He'd occasionally glance up from the newspaper to check out his surroundings. So far, at least, everything appeared to be going smoothly. There was the usual lunchtime crowd crisscrossing the park, in the main, office workers out for a breath of relatively fresh air and a bite to eat.

A mother and child walking an excitable fluffy white poodle briefly caught his attention. The girl was screeching with delight as she played with the cute new addition to their family. Following their progress along the path, Spencer developed a wistful, almost bemused smile. There were times when he longed for nothing more than to break free from the constant pressure and endless grind of leading a covert existence, but, like Joyce, he'd probably end up kicking his heels and end up becoming bored to death.

He glanced at the newspaper, his mind wandering back to his invitation he had received from Cavendish to visit *HMS Dolphin* and the mini submarines designed to provide the West with intelligence on the Soviet's 14th Submarine Squadron. Spencer had suspected the invite had been nothing more than a cynical ploy to extend an olive branch between their respective sister organisations. It was a time when Cavendish had undoubtedly already compromised the top-secret operation and the lives of the young submariners, who would have been sent to their deaths.

Countless hours and taxpayer's money had been ploughed into the project and all for nothing. The British government might as well have flushed the entire bloody lot down the nearest available sewer. Every plan and scientific detail had been gifted to the Soviets.

As arranged, at precisely one o'clock, Spencer caught sight of the unmistakably suave, languid figure of Sir Dick Cavendish entering the park via Piccadilly. On first impressions, Cavendish looked rather more like an erudite professor than a master spy. He paused, taking an inordinate amount of time adjusting his trademark trilby hat and re-arranging a maroon silk scarf draped casually around his neck against the biting wind.

Having fastidiously sorted out his attire, Cavendish carefully appraised his surroundings before unhurriedly sauntering his way across the park. Outwardly, he seemed not to have a care in the world. He stopped to casually tease a cigarette from a slender engraved case, languidly slipping it into his mouth and flicking on a matching lighter. He then proceeded to make his way through the park, the cigarette poised lightly between his fingers, occasionally taking the odd puff.

Spotting Spencer on a bench, Cavendish decided to take a shortcut across the grass to join him.

Spencer glanced up from his newspaper and carefully folded it. 'Dick, thank you for coming at such short notice.'

Cavendish inclined his head slightly and joined him on the bench. 'My dear chap, I don't know about you, but I'm getting just a little too long in the tooth, and *senior*, to be playing cat and mouse!'

'Yes, me too,' Spencer conceded with a perfunctory smile.

'What the hell's going on? Are you sure it can't have waited? I've had to cancel lunch at the Guard's Club.' His voice was irritable and faintly bored. 'I really don't have time for this kind of unconventional...'

'I just thought it might be a little easier this way,' Spencer cut in.

Cavendish's pale grey eyes fixed on him with the merest hint of curiosity. 'Whatever it damn well is, I hope it's not going to take too long. I have a meeting with the Foreign Secretary at two!' He paused to take a long draw on the cigarette. 'So, what's all this bloody nonsense about?'

For a while, Spencer sat stone-faced, unresponsive. 'Have you ever come across a Soviet agent called Wolf?'

Cavendish looked vaguely perplexed. 'Other than the four-legged variety, no, I can't say as I have, dear chap. The fact you've dragged me out of a warm office to this godforsaken park, I can only assume you think it's important?'

Spencer folded his arms. 'Well, I'm not sure about you, Dick, but I'm personally not into playing mind games.'

'Forgive me. I didn't know we were,' Cavendish drawled, his gaze drifting idly across the park. 'I see you've decided to come mob-handed,' he said, inclining his head toward Spencer's bodyguards, who retained a respectful distance.

'Come on, Dick, I think we both know why they're here.'

'And what might that be?'

'I take it that *I'm* addressing Agent Wolf?'

Cavendish's faintly bored expression didn't falter. 'Wolf? What in God's name are you prattling on about, man!'

'You could say, Jack Stein has handed me a smoking gun.'

The older spymaster's brows suddenly furrowed, a scowl forming. 'What kind of smoking gun?'

'A CIA report containing the name of the KGB's top double agent operating here in the UK…it was yours, Dick.'

Cavendish's silence was answer enough. He also now realised why he'd only discovered Stein had arrived in London after a chance conversation with a relatively junior member of his staff, who had bumped into the CIA's Deputy Director in the St Philip's foyer. At the time, Cavendish really hadn't read too much into it. However, in hindsight, it was unusual he had not received word of Stein's arrival in the UK.

Cavendish had no real idea how much the CIA had on him, but knew Spencer would never have dared move an inch without being sure of his ground.

'I can only assume Vasiliev and the Politburo view you as their number one apostle!' Spencer said tetchily.

There was a protracted silence between them before Cavendish answered with an air of resignation, 'Perhaps they do, who knows. But, I suppose, I should count myself lucky,' Cavendish announced unexpectedly.

'What the hell makes you say that?'

'Well, my dear chap, in your younger days, you'd probably have shot me on the spot and asked questions later.'

'There's no *probably* about it. Believe me, *Dick*, if I thought I could still get away with it...'

'There's no need to explain yourself,' Cavendish mused with a shadow of a smile.

However, beneath the accomplished, polished

façade, he was a broken man. He clasped hands tightly, staring vacantly out across the park.

Had they perhaps managed to link him to his former MI6 colleagues – Burgess, Maclean, and Blake – all of whom had been outed as Soviet agents? God, if only he hadn't been tempted out of retirement. Rather than facing disgrace and sitting in a chilly London park, right now, he would probably be enjoying a round of golf at his club and living out his days as a respected former Chief of the Service.

Even so, he suspected that if Vasiliev hadn't been hell-bent on settling a blood score against Ivanov, and handled everything in a timely and professional manner, he might, just might, have remained under the radar. There had simply been no reason to rush things. But after ordering the assassination of Ivanov on British soil, his own position had become increasingly untenable. The KGB's chief was a man whose increasingly erratic behaviour and lack of professionalism was now endangering the lives of many people like himself, who had loyally served the Soviet Union and communism for many years.

During his time at Cambridge University, Cavendish had been a willing recruit to the communist cause and had joined his good friend, and subsequent intelligence colleague, Guy Burgess. But long before their recruitment, Cavendish was already dedicated to the ideology of Marxism.

At the height of World War II, he'd never viewed his work against Fascism as a problem. Spying for Britain and America's Russian ally against Nazism had seemed to him a patriotic duty to pass information to the Russians. However, post-war, like his fellow double agents, he'd never ceased leaking state secrets to Moscow Central.

Cavendish had devoted himself body and soul to the cause. After Burgess's discovery, suspicion was rampant across the entire Service. But he was all too aware those feelings would be magnified a thousand times over when news of his own betrayal came to light.

'Before the war,' Cavendish said rather waspishly, almost as if thinking aloud, 'the Soviets made it their business to target young, idealistic, disaffected members of society…key intellectuals.'

Spencer grunted derisively.

Cavendish looked at him sharply.

'I've heard you described as many things, Dick, but never an *intellectual*!'

A slight smug expression crossed Cavendish's face. 'Isn't that a bit rich coming from a *grammar* schoolboy?'

'I've never claimed to be an intellectual, far from it, besides they'd have found me out years ago!'

'I don't mind telling you, Spencer, your appointment as DG sent shock waves throughout the Service,' Cavendish said with barely disguised disdain.

'I think you'll find it was meant to,' came the considered response.

'Really?'

'The government appointed me for one reason, and one reason only, to root out the malaise and the corruption in *your* ruddy department.'

He began chuckling softly. 'Well, you certainly missed me, dear boy, didn't you?' His voice was low and edged with bitterness.

'I'll put that down to a case of misplaced loyalty and trust,' came the equally sharp response. 'What's past is past. But you've finally reached the end of the line, Dick. It's over!'

After being dragged out of retirement, Cavendish had adroitly played the game of steering MI6 away from the often-suffocating constraints of Whitehall's powerful mandarins, and in particular, the Prime Minister, while at the same time re-engaging with his demoralised department.

Spencer had initially agreed with many of his views and potential reforms. Still, it was only now with the luxury of hindsight, Spencer realised, that Cavendish's duplicitous approach was both hard-nosed and savvy.

'I'm assuming another public trial would be just a little too painful for Her Majesty's government?' Cavendish's voice was an irritating mix of sarcasm and smugness.

Spencer took his time in answering his once-trusted colleague. 'Yes, apparently so,' he said quietly. 'The powers that be have unfortunately decided to offer you immunity from prosecution in exchange for your full cooperation.'

Cavendish smiled, blowing away a little smoke. 'You mean, in exchange for giving up everything I know?'

Spencer inclined his head. 'Well, that's *their* theory. It certainly wasn't my decision.'

'No, I can imagine it wasn't.' Figuring he didn't have anything to lose, Cavendish decided to bluff it out a little longer. He folded his arms and took a deep breath. 'So apart from this "Wolf" business, what exactly do our American cousins believe they have on me?'

'It's not just the CIA, Dick; otherwise, I wouldn't be bloody sitting here.'

'I suppose not,' he murmured vaguely.

'In February of 1951, you made the first of several visits that year to the MI6 Station in Berlin.'

Cavendish arched his brows curiously. 'What if I did?'

'You became friendly—well...*friendly* is probably for want of a better word—with a young CIA officer called Chuck Faulkner.'

If it struck a chord with MI6's spy chief, he was still giving nothing away.

'It was during this period you were placed in contact with another by *your* Soviet handler.' Spencer passed him a long hard cold look, before asking sarcastically, 'Has that helped to refresh your memory any?'

Cavendish compressed his lips before throwing him a half-hearted smile. 'No, I can't say as it has,' he lied evenly. 'I've met Faulkner, of course, but that, let's see, was at least two years or so ago when I did a stint in the US. At the time, I'm convinced the Service didn't quite know what to do with me. I was heading for retirement, and...well, given my seniority, in time honoured fashion, they decided to send me off on a rather nice sabbatical to study our intelligence gathering with our American cousins. I really rather enjoyed myself,' Cavendish said smugly.

'But Langley certainly wasn't the first time you met him, *was it?* Chuck Faulkner or Elvin, as he was known at the time, worked out of the CIA's headquarters in Frankfurt.'

Cavendish was surprised; they had even managed to confirm a link to Faulkner. He hadn't seen the ruddy man in years, and until they'd been reunited in the US, he really hadn't followed his career path with any great interest; there was simply no need. He'd almost forgotten about him until shortly before his posting to the States, when a report had landed on his desk naming Faulkner as the new boss overseeing the CIA's operations against the Soviet Union. It was a pretty impressive accolade. After their initial meetings in Germany, their respective careers had been deliberately stove-piped by Moscow Central. At the time of his appointment, Cavendish recalled feeling faintly surprised and could only hope that Faulkner had tightened up his act. Still, either way, with Cavendish's posting to the CIA's HQ, it was a significant coup for Vasiliev, who probably couldn't quite believe his luck.

Back in Frankfurt, the then young, sometimes pushy, ambitious CIA officer hadn't struck him as the slickest of operators. However, for whatever reason, Vasiliev had considered him useful. He had been proved right, of course. Looking back, neither of them had particularly impressed him. Both were both equally guilty of being a little too free and easy with their methods, but had simply put it down to inexperience, and that they were still learning their craft.

Eleven years down the line, they had all moved on, but one man, in his opinion, still hadn't quite grasped the concept. Without Khrushchev's patronage, Vasiliev would never have headed up the KGB.

As Spencer continued, his slick matter-of-fact delivery of the case against him, Cavendish's glib, hardened carapace expression was steadily beginning to melt away. Up until now, he'd been fortunate, in so much as his pre-eminence within the intelligence community had provided him with a degree of immunity; that he was somehow above suspicion and therefore almost entirely untouchable.

However, bit by bit, the one man he had always feared in the Service was clinically tearing both the façade and his reputation apart. It was almost akin to a verbal laceration of *Lingchi*, the ancient Chinese method of execution, a death by a thousand cuts.

For the Americans, the toxic poison created by Faulkner's betrayal was colossal, but no less than his own. Perhaps it was always inevitable he would be found out in the end. But the shame of being confronted face-to-face by his old nemesis somehow made it all the more embarrassing. The game was up. There was nowhere else to hide, leaving his former colleagues counting the cost of his double life.

'One man's hero is another's traitor,' he offered up. Even to Cavendish's mind, his response had sounded rather inane and compounded his unease.

Spencer looked through, rather than at him. 'Have you ever seriously asked yourself how much damage you've done to the Service? And how many of *our* agents you've sent to their deaths?'

It was an interesting question, and one he hadn't thought about before. Cavendish found himself making a mental tally. His best estimate, he announced without a shred of emotion, was probably close to perhaps three or four hundred agents. He wasn't entirely sure. It could well have been more.

Spencer held back a while, struggling to keep a grip. Vengeance was a dish best served cold and could wait for another day. 'Why did you have Bradley killed?' he managed to ask evenly.

'Because he was becoming a bloody nuisance, that's why! You should never have taken him on in the first place. He was a novice; he got in the way.'

'You mean he got in *your* way?

Cavendish grunted derisively. 'Hardly!'

'So, Bradley was onto you?'

'He was a nosy little shit and too clever for his

own good!' Cavendish snapped, flicking his spent cigarette onto the path and carefully adjusted his silk scarf. Easing himself off the bench, his gaze roamed across the park.

'I take it *your* people are here to escort me?' he queried, inclining his head toward Spencer's smartly dressed officers.

'Yes, they are.'

'Then, with your permission, I'd like to collect a few personal items from the office.'

'Give me a list, and we'll take care of it.'

'As you wish.'

Cavendish started to retrace his steps when Spencer's voice cut through him like a knife. 'I've drafted your resignation letter; I want a signed copy on my desk by first thing tomorrow morning.'

In response, a slow, twisted smile surfaced across his face. 'Don't worry; you'll have it. But if I were you, Spencer, I'd keep a very close eye on *your* Russian lackey. I understand on good authority you never quite know what you're getting with Comrade Ivanov!'

It was a vitriolic aside, but one Cavendish hoped might seed yet another root of doubt in Spencer's mind. He again re-adjusted his scarf, it was a nervous gesture, before heading back out of the park shadowed by MI5 officers.

After tendering his resignation, the system would deliver the ultimate humiliation. Two separately enciphered telegrams would be cabled to the heads of every MI6 Station across the world, caveated for their eyes only. The first blunt message would read:

The following name is a Traitor.

The second would contain nine letters. After deciphering the message from London, it would spell out:

C-A-V-E-N-D-I-S-H

The cable would send shockwaves throughout the Service. Despite his seemingly indifferent performance, the shame and guilt of his actions weighed heavily upon him. Still, perhaps the greatest ignominy was knowing his security files would end up being stamped in bold red ink with "Sov-Bloc Red" the damning confirmation he was a traitor. For some reason, it rankled with him that some junior Central Registry clerk would see him for what he was and maliciously share his disgrace with their colleagues.

Unbeknown to Cavendish, the Prime Minister had instructed the cable was to be signed off by Spencer. His intention was both clear and calculated. It was meant to send out a warning shot that if things didn't radically improve, the PM intended to bring Britain's overseas intelligence arm into line, and without due compliance, wouldn't hesitate to merge the two agencies into one.

While Spencer had felt faintly flattered by the PM's decision, he'd made it clear from the outset the ensuing fallout of any potential merger of MI5 with MI6 was, in his view, little more than an academic exercise. But if the PM was deadly serious about seeing it through to the end, it was way more than he'd be willing to accept and would offer his resignation.

Following his colleague's progress across the park, Spencer burned with anger and a deep sense of personal betrayal. It was also a national travesty. Although Cavendish certainly wasn't a lone "Wolf" in the ranks of British Intelligence, he had been at the epicentre of their cabal of betrayal. There were others...other names he hadn't yet tracked down, but who like Cavendish's hands were drenched in blood.

The strands of loyalty that had once seemingly bound them together were lost forever and had never been more than a fragile charade of smoking mirrors.

CHAPTER 23

No.10 Downing Street
Westminster, London

After returning from Bradley's funeral, Prime Minister Hawley was in full flow on the front steps of No.10, holding court addressing a large gaggle of Fleet Street and international hacks.

As if on cue, as the cameras rolled, so did his tears. All in all, even his harshest critics, and there were many, agreed it was a bravura performance from a usually uptight British politician. Whether the sudden outpouring of emotion was genuine remained somewhat open to conjecture.

In the wake of the press coverage, his harshest critics would as always be quick to pass judgement, suggesting the PM's talents might well be better served on the West End stage, rather than Parliament.

On the other hand, Spencer suspected his

supporters would come out fighting, viewing his heartfelt response to the world's press as a mark of the man. Loyal and empathetic to the core.

The truth probably lay somewhere betwixt the bitter polarisation of both factions.

While Hawley continued to milk the media's attention, Spencer slipped quietly through the rear entrance of the Prime Minister's official London residence.

Inside No.10 lurked a veritable hotchpotch of spaces cobbled together over many years as the need to expand the original house and terrace steadily increased with the growing demands of successive governments.

Spencer was greeted on the back stairs by the Prime Minister's private secretary, Mike Beardmore. Tall and lean in stature, he always looked slightly anaemic and in need of a good hearty meal. Whatever his dietary needs may or may not have been, he was always unfailingly polite. However, Spencer had never particularly warmed to the man. He found the loud booming voice and frequently forced laughter faintly boorish.

While Spencer didn't necessarily share some of the wilder opinions circulating Whitehall about the Prime Minister's right-hand man, in Westminster terms, he viewed Beardmore as being somewhat second-rate. He was perhaps a surprising choice for the crucial role of private secretary, when there were far more talented and able candidates the PM could have picked.

Beardmore was viewed amongst his peers as possessing all the emotional spectrum of a block of ice. He was also renowned for having an opinion on just about everyone and everything. His barbed observations were invariably peppered with an almost sneering, none-too-subtle vindictive malevolence. As a result, Beardmore's outbursts consistently proved somewhat divisive amongst the Prime Minister's parliamentary colleagues. Around Whitehall he was known as the sort of man who would knife you in the back – and then report you for carrying a concealed weapon.

In Spencer's opinion, Beardmore wasn't a details man and had often found himself wanting during meetings. But boorish or not, the fact he had the Prime Minister's ear continued to make him a force to be reckoned with.

By the time they reached the PM's office, Hawley had, as a consequence, only just returned from facing the press outside No.10. He was tilted back in a comfortable leather chair, attired in one of his customary hand-stitched three-piece suits, and was loosening his equally immaculately knotted black tie.

'Spencer, please come on in and take a seat,' he said effusively.

Their meetings were usually a hard slog, so it was unusual to find Hawley in a reasonably half-decent mood. Spencer could only surmise it was probably down to his impromptu interview, which seemed to have gone down well received by the press.

'Thanks, Mike.'

Beardmore inclined his head and smiled in response before leaving them alone.

'I hope it wasn't too much of a circus today, sir?' Spencer asked politely before taking a seat across the desk.

'No, thank God, it wasn't,' he said, taking an intake of breath. 'Given everything that's been going on lately, you never quite know how these things are going to pan out.'

'Well, at least the press didn't gate-crash the funeral.'

'Yes. My only concern was for Bradley's family. They've been through so much already.'

'I only wish I had been able to pay my respects.'

Hawley looked faintly surprised. The serpentine glint, which was never far from the surface, flashed in the heavy-lidded hazel eyes. '*Really?*' he said, swaying side to side in the swivel chair. 'Bradley's parents requested a private funeral...only close family and friends. Somehow, Spencer, under the circumstances, I really don't think it would have been entirely appropriate, do you?'

Spencer appeared nonplussed. 'I'm sorry, why ever not?'

Hawley peered across at him, squinting, scanning his face. 'Surely you can't be serious? For god sake, man, if it hadn't been for your sordid, grubby, little schemes, Bradley would still be alive! Why on earth would his family want *you*, of all people, at the church? Believe me, Spencer, it was difficult enough discovering Bradley was murdered by some bloody, lunatic Russian hitman, let alone that he was working for your ruddy lot!'

'Well, that's one way of looking at it, sir.' Spencer smiled enigmatically.

Closing his eyes in exasperation, Hawley tried collecting his thoughts. He'd long since realised it was frequently far wiser to keep a cool head when dealing with MI5's Director-General. By choice, he'd far rather have dispensed with his services altogether and picked someone far easier to work with. But he had erred on the side of caution.

In fairness, he knew Spencer had served his predecessors with unbiased neutrality, and in turn, they sought his advice. Hawley knew he was an honest broker, and given the catastrophe surrounding Cavendish, his undeniable influence and standing behind the scenes had navigated a way to make a deal with his CIA friends. But had, by default, helped keep the lines of communication open with their respective governments while avoiding the usual somewhat slow diplomatic channels. In many ways, it had been a masterclass of under the counter diplomacy. Even so, Hawley still felt a little uneasy about it all. At heart, Spencer was a maverick; it had worked this time, but what if it hadn't?

Hawley began tapping the tip of his pen against the edge of the desk, accompanied by a slightly distracting nervous twitch in his right eye.

Spencer quietly smiled. The somewhat annoying habit only ever manifested itself when Hawley was under extreme stress. He'd often wondered how a psychiatrist might view the PM's nervous tic; it fleetingly crossed Spencer's mind the analysis would probably be worth more than its weight in gold.

'Do we have an update from Garvan?' Hawley asked.

Spencer assumed the PM was referring to the attack on Ivanov's convoy. 'Yes, we do, sir.'

'And?'

'I was under the impression Garvan's report was handed by Scotland Yard to Beardmore.'

'Yes…yes, that's right

Digging a little deeper, Hawley recalled, if somewhat vaguely, reading that a couple of Russians. Along with one of Garvan's officers, whose name he couldn't quite recall, had died during the attack on the convoy.

'It was Lew Lillywhite,' Spencer cut in, irritably.

Feeling faintly embarrassed, the PM thanked him before hurriedly slipping on his reading glasses, he snatched the CIA's report from his in-tray, caveated for "the PM's eyes only".

Hawley regularly relied heavily on a mixture of trusted civil service staff and a few well-chosen, political acolytes to carry out the routine day-to-day donkey work for him. Highlighting the relevant bullet points of his massive in-tray without getting too bogged down in the nitty-gritty. In Whitehall, there was a much often quoted saying amongst his parliamentary colleagues that Hawley was never wrong, never sorry, and never responsible.

Judging by the number of dog-eared pages, Spencer guessed it was probably the first official document the PM had ever actually read through from cover to cover.

Hawley pulled off his glasses. 'How exactly do we stand with the Soviets? They must know Egorov and Bobrik are dead, so why the silence?'

'What would you do in their shoes?'

'Well, that's just it, Spencer, to be perfectly frank with you, I'm not entirely sure how I'd play it,' he admitted. He began tapping his pen against the edge of his desk again. 'I don't know about you, but I was certainly expecting something to come out of the woodwork after we shipped the Stasi officers back to Germany. But there hasn't been a bloody peep out of East Berlin or Moscow, for that matter!'

'I'd probably have been more surprised if there had. The Stasi officers were nothing more than stooges, a means to an end.'

'I presume Cavendish was behind the attack on the convoy?'

Spencer inclined his head.

'Can we guarantee Ivanov's safety at the estate?'

'Only time will tell, sir. As you know, two of the hit squad are still at large.' Spencer said bluntly. 'The estate's on lockdown, but then again, so was the mews house.'

Hawley began flicking through the file and without looking up, asked, 'I understand you've had a meeting with Dick Cavendish.'

'Yes, earlier this afternoon. I've ordered him to have his signed resignation on my desk first thing tomorrow morning.'

'Hmm, we really need to keep a tight lid on things. We can't afford any of this stuff to leak out.'

Spencer agreed with him.

'I believe his deputy, General Sinden, has been lined up to take over, is that right?'

'Yes, sir, he has.'

'Then make sure it's only a temporary fix!'

Spencer looked faintly surprised.

'I've never been overly impressed by the man!' Hawley continued. 'He's too old school, too tainted for my liking.'

'You mean guilt by association?'

'No, not entirely. In my opinion, Spencer, he's simply not up to the job!' he grunted, before abruptly changing the subject. 'Will Cavendish cooperate?'

'I've no idea; we'll have to wait and see.'

'Then I suggest you'd better start cranking up the pressure on the old bastard!' Noting Spencer's slightly puzzled expression, he asked impatiently, 'Is anything wrong?'

'Well, that all rather depends on whether or not we're talking off the record.'

'Why wouldn't we be?'

For once, Spencer was inclined to believe him.

Like most politicians, he was driven by self-preservation, and in Hawley's case, was accompanied by a need to analyse every word to the nth degree.

Stretching back in his chair, Hawley folded his arms, almost defensively. 'You have my word; *it's strictly off the record!*' he emphasised. 'I can't help thinking that on paper, your Soviet friend, Ivanov, looks like the best thing since sliced bread.' He paused for effect; his face contorted into a half-smile. 'I don't know about you, Spencer, but in my experience, if something looks too good to be true, then it generally is.' Hawley started toying with his glasses again. 'If Comrade Ivanov was as slick as you've led me to believe, then why the hell didn't he pick up on Cavendish?'

'Perhaps Vasiliev deliberately kept him out of the loop.'

Hawley rolled his eyes. 'But you're not sure?'

'We need more time,' came the bleak response.

'We already have enough excess baggage of our own; I don't want any more trouble, Spencer.'

'No, sir.'

'So, what are you going to do with him?'

'Fly him off to Canada.'

Hawley's expression registered surprise. 'When?'

'If all goes according to plan, tomorrow evening from RAF Northolt.'

'Why Canada?' he quizzed.

'The original plan was for Ivanov to remain here in the UK under an assumed name. Sadly, Cavendish has made that all but virtually impossible.'

'I'd have thought the obvious choice was America.'

'You've read the report, sir, they already have more than enough on their plate at the moment with Faulkner, let alone playing nanny to Ivanov.'

'Yes, I can see that.' Hawley placed the flat of his hand on the CIA report. 'Tell me something,' he queried warily. 'It's just a thought, but I do hope to God you've discussed all of this with the Foreign Office. I mean, that you've come to some deal or other with Canadian Intelligence?'

Spencer passed him a slight smile. 'Yes, I have. As for the FO, they'll know about it as soon as you've briefed them.'

Hawley physically groaned in despair. 'I wish you'd bloody well said something to me about all this earlier! I mean, what the hell were you thinking about going it alone?'

'It was a case of parallel diplomacy,' he said by way of explanation.

'Really, is *that* what you call it!'

'To be perfectly honest with you, sir, I really didn't have the time or the patience to deal with the FO's endless red tape. If we had, Ivanov might well have been stuck here for the next six months.'

Hawley screwed up his face sympathetically. 'Six months if you were lucky.'

'I also wasn't entirely sure who I could trust.'

'Yes, I get it,' Hawley said dourly. The links between the Foreign Office and Cavendish's arm of the Service were inseparable. 'And what about the Canadian government? How on earth have you managed to persuade them to give Ivanov political asylum? They can't have taken him on board lightly.'

'My sources have assured me they're on-side.'

'Well, for all our sakes, let's hope they are!' Hawley peered pointedly over their half-moon lenses at his small brass desk clock. It was a subliminal message; their meeting was at an end. 'I guess we should start thinking about winding things up.'

'Of course, I'll be in touch,' Spencer said, pushing his chair back.

As he made his way out of the office, Hawley called after him. Releasing his grip of the door handle, he spun around.

'I have a feeling you've already been briefed by your American *cousins* that I'm expecting a call from the White House.'

Spencer smiled. 'I couldn't possibly comment, sir.'

Hawley let out a roll of laughter. For once, it was entirely genuine. 'I'd be almost disappointed if you didn't know! Before I speak with the President, is there *anything* else I should know about?'

'Not that I can think of.'

'The CIA's report mentioned that Mirsky had managed to get a hook on Vasiliev. I was just wondering exactly how much dirt the Americans have on him. I mean, is it enough to bring the man down?'

'Hard to say. We're not even sure if Moscow will buy it.'

'Ah, for once, Spencer, I actually believe you've given me an honest answer.' Hawley smirked.

A faint trace of a smile etched across his face in response. 'As I said, Prime Minister, I'll be in touch.'

CHAPTER 24

RAF Northolt
North West London

At 0830 hours, a small four-seater aircraft piloted by a former Fleet Air Arm officer, Jock Weir, rolled slowly along the taxiway as a Canadian military transporter roared overhead.

'I reckon that's probably your one, boss,' Weir said in his soft Edinburgh burr.

Spencer glanced out of the side window as an impressive military plane thundered down the runaway with a screech of brakes and the rubber of smoking tyres in its wake.

'If it isn't, Jock, I'm screwed,' he laughed.

Weir chuckled, bringing them to a halt, waiting for the okay from the control to take off.

The Canadian transporter's arrival was validation that his gamble had finally paid off. In opting to reach out to Jake Moore, his opposite number in the Canadian Security Service, rather than the Foreign Office, to facilitate negotiations had been a calculated risk, which could have seriously backfired. At first, his approach to Moore had appeared to be little more than an informal back-channel beneath their respective diplomatic radars. He hadn't wanted to come in hard, but merely floated a few ideas. Besides, Spencer knew Moore was someone he could do business with.

Even though, avoiding the minutiae of Foreign Office red tape had helped to speed things up, it had still taken hours of delicate behind the scenes negotiations before the Canadian Government was finally persuaded to be brought onboard. Perhaps understandably, they'd initially viewed accepting responsibility for Ivanov as little more than a poisoned chalice and had taken it right to the wire before Moore's political masters had agreed to accept him.

Having been given the green light, the Canadian High Commission in Trafalgar Square duly issued the relevant paperwork for Ivanov's new life. Citizenship was granted, along with a passport under an assumed name, complete with a watertight back story.

The arrival of the military transporter was the final piece of the jigsaw and was scheduled to return across the Atlantic with its precious Soviet cargo at 1930 hours.

After the deadly attack on the convoy, Spencer

had opted for Weir to take the four-seater down to the Southwater Estate, collect Ivanov, and then hand him over to the Canadians back at Northolt.

Weir continued to keep the four-seater's engine idling over; there were several RAF planes ahead of them waiting to take off. Spencer had flown with the Scotsman before. He was a small, slim dapper-looking man, who was always impeccably dressed, with his customary pristine white shirt, carefully knotted paisley cravat, and cavalry twill trousers.

As a former Fleet Air Arm experimental test pilot, based at the Royal Aircraft Establishment in Farnborough, Weir was far more accustomed to flying leading edge jet fighters and landing on aircraft carriers than handling a single prop plane.

There had been the odd occasion when Spencer had the distinct impression the bugger was flying by the seat of his pants and, out of sheer boredom, was putting the tiny prop through its paces just for the hell of it. Right or wrong, in Spencer's experience, Weir always flew like that and probably knew no other way.

During World War II, Northolt had served as a base for both the RAF and the so-called free Polish Air Force squadron. Throughout hostilities, it had also served as the home of Winston Churchill's personal plane. Ever since the war, British Intelligence had continued to retain two light aircraft at the base on permanent standby. There was a small, specially selected mix of both serving and ex-RAF and Royal

Navy pilots on the duty roster. Weir's wartime experience flying a raft of covert missions, plus his subsequent renown as a test pilot, had made him a natural choice to be invited to join the team.

At the time, Weir hadn't hesitated to accept their offer and viewed his duties for the Service as not only a distraction from the day job, but almost as an additional adrenaline fix.

On receiving clearance from the tower for take-off, Weir acknowledged the call before re-confirming and repeating the instruction over to the air traffic controller. He then glanced casually across the cockpit. 'Are you ready, boss?'

Spencer inclined his head. 'Ready as I'll ever be, I suppose.'

'I'll have you there in a jiffy.'

'Don't worry yourself, Jock. Take as long as you like, just as long as you get me there one piece!'

'Aye, right!' Weir laughed, rotating the controls sending the tiny plane hurtling at full speed down the runway.

With the prop engine roaring, they were soon in the air before banking sharply into their flight path. In less than an hour, they were flying over the undulating patchwork terrain of the Surrey Hills, with its rolling chalk downs, boxed woodland, and heaths, before slowly beginning their descent across the county border into Sussex toward the vast sprawling Southwater estate.

As they approached, the sky was a dark leaden

grey, and a fine mist of rain swept across the parkland. Although Weir had studied the flight plan in meticulous detail, given the torrential overnight downpour of rain and never having landed at the estate before, he decided to err on the side of caution and recce the lay of the land before committing himself to land.

After several circuits of the estate and its impressive Tudor mansion, Weir didn't fancy running the risk of upending the plane on the perfectly manicured, but sodden lawns and opted to bring them down on the driveway. However, it was flanked by a dense canopy of elm trees, and it certainly wasn't an ideal choice.

As they skimmed over the curved, red-bricked chimney stacks, Spencer let out a stream of expletives. He was by no means a nervous flyer. In his time, he'd survived his fair share of close shaves, but Weir's instinctively skilful, albeit occasionally gung-ho approach, occasionally got the better of him, sending the pit of his stomach into his mouth.

'Anything wrong, boss?' Weir queried, glancing across the cockpit.

'What the hell you are you playing at!' he groaned, the tension in his voice rising.

'I can't risk us landing on the lawn, boss; it's saturated.'

'I don't care about the bloody lawns, Jock; we're in touching distance of the effing roof!

'It can't be helped,' Weir said calmly.

'So, where *are* we going?'

'The driveway,' Weir smiled, banking sharply.

In a bid to avoid the overhanging branches, they began descending steeply.

'For God's sake, Jock, just land the effing thing, *will you!*' came the clipped response.

'Aye, boss,' he said, carefully lowering the nose of the plane between the avenue of elm trees before landing smoothly on the driveway and taxiing to a halt outside the mansion's entrance.

'Are you gonna fly back with us to Northolt, boss?' Weir asked, killing the engine.

'No. At my age, Jock, I can only take so much excitement in one day,' he said half-jokingly.

Weir laughed almost to himself. His brief had been kept deliberately tight, other than knowing there was to be a handover of a spy at Northolt to the Canadians. Apart from the flight plan, and the fact the *boss* needed to be flown down to the Southwater estate, he was pretty much in the dark.

CHAPTER 25

Southwater Estate, Horsham
West Sussex, England

Heading up the stairs, Spencer asked Joyce whether she'd had a chance to read his security brief about Dick Cavendish.

She screwed her face in disgust. 'Yes, I have. Where is he now?'

'At home.'

Joyce looked disappointed; placing him under house arrest in all but name seemed way too good for someone who had betrayed not only the Service, but the entire country.

'I have a feeling *good old Dickie* will take most of his secrets and lies to the grave,' she said bitterly.

'Maybe, but at least he won't take all of 'em!'

'Even so, isn't it a bit like closing the ruddy stable door after the horse has bolted.'

Spencer turned to face her on the landing. 'It is what it is, Jo.'

Joyce held his gaze. 'And so we're simply going to bury the story as if nothing happened?'

'It's out of our hands, Jo. It's the government's call. To be perfectly honest with you, for once, I'm in agreement with the PM. The Service's reputation has already been dragged through the mud more than enough lately. It was bad enough with Maclean, but think about it, Jo. We'd never recover if it were made public MI6's Chief was a long-standing Soviet agent. We need to draw a line under it; mend bridges with our allies and move on.'

'But the bastard very nearly had us all killed!' Joyce snapped back at him.

'There's no point in shooting the messenger, Jo,' he said quietly, continuing up the staircase.

'No, I guess not,' she apologised, following him. 'Do you believe Cavendish was behind Bradley's murder?'

'Well, I'd be more surprised if he wasn't!'

<hr>

Having watched the small light aircraft land on the driveway, Ivanov drew himself away from the sash window, a freshly lit Gauloises draped casually in the corner of his mouth, and perched himself on the arm of a Chesterfield sofa. The prospect of facing

Spencer again, after their somewhat terse encounter at the mews house, had been on his mind.

Long before Ivanov had defected, his life was already on the line. Still, he had never expected Spencer, of all people, would question whether or not he'd been stringing British Intelligence along and playing a double-bluff with them.

Perhaps he had nothing to worry about. Joyce had already assured him Spencer's visit was simply a mark of his importance to the government. Mercurial by nature, Joyce wasn't exactly an open book, and he never quite knew whether or not she was lying to him. It was practically impossible to read or penetrate the deadpan exterior.

Ivanov was almost swayed to buy her explanation, hook, line, and sinker, but sensed something serious had happened; that things weren't quite right between his minders. Ivanov had a great deal of time for Lewis. He was understated and affable to a fault; they got on easily. He was comfortable to be with. However, the deceptive softness in his tone and manner had changed almost imperceptibly, barely masking an unexpected seriousness when he spoke.

Unlike Lewis, Carter was far more difficult to gauge. His six-foot frame and muscular body were impressive enough, and he was usually the life and soul of the group. Again, like his colleagues, over the last forty-eight hours, there was a marked difference in his demeanour.

Hearing the door click open, Ivanov turned expectantly. Spencer entered alone. He looked strained.

'Good flight?' Ivanov enquired politely.

'I've had better!' came the prickly response, as he dumped a surprisingly battered attaché case on an armchair.

He retrieved a key from his trouser pocket, unlocked it, and produced a large manila coloured envelope. 'Here, take this,' he said, handing it over.

Ivanov raised his eyes questioningly.

'You'll find everything you need in there. Passport, identity papers, background stuff.'

Ivanov thanked him. 'I'm surprised the Canadians agreed to take me on board.'

'Let's put it this way; it certainly wasn't easy.' Spencer smiled.

'No, I imagine it can't have been. But thank you,' Ivanov said, opening the envelope.

'You'll be flown to Trenton Air Force base this evening from Northolt.'

'Trenton?'

'It's in Ontario,' Spencer explained, setting the attaché case on the floor and easing himself back into the armchair. He began patting his jacket pockets searching for his Craven A cigarettes, and produced an unopened pack, laying them on the side table. 'Tell me something, Alexei, have you ever come across an agent called Wolf before?'

Ivanov pursed his lips. 'No, I'm sorry, I can't say that I have.'

'Interesting,' he said, picking up the cigarettes, and began slowly unwrapping the cellophane around the packet.

Ivanov stared back at him curiously. 'Should I know them?' he countered.

'Well, that's just the point, Alexei. Up until a few days ago, Wolf was the KGB's top double agent operating out of the UK.'

He narrowed his eyes, looking confused. 'There's gotta be some kind of mistake, I mean…'

'I assure you, Alexei, there hasn't been a mistake!'

Ivanov realised he was in a no-win situation, and no matter what he said, or did, Spencer was unlikely to be convinced of his innocence. His heart started thudding violently, his thoughts racing. Now at least, he understood why the sudden mood change of his MI5 minders. The sudden shift in mood, the British government undoubtedly now viewed him as a liability. Perhaps that was the real reason behind their decision to ship him off to Canada? If he were lucky, he'd probably end his days in some snowbound godforsaken place, with little more than the odd brown bear and caribou for company. The food and the treatment might well be better than a Siberian Gulag, but he hated long, cold winters.

An impending sense of dread swept over him. He was battling for his life on more than one front.

Even before Spencer's arrival, Ivanov had always known that once he'd defected and was out of the spying game, with time, it was inevitable both his knowledge and usefulness would eventually become increasingly redundant to the West.

His value and reputation as a double agent were only ever as good as his last intelligence report. Ivanov had willingly run the risk of expendability, but now, it was facing him full on and in a way he had never quite imagined it would.

Spencer lit a cigarette before reaching down into his attaché case, rummaging around inside he finally produced a flimsy piece of signal paper. 'Read this!' he said, proffering it.

Ivanov hesitated before stepping forward to take it. The wording was stark, coldly clinical, and to the point in the naming and shaming of Sir Richard Cavendish as a Soviet traitor. As the last vestige of colour drained from his face, Ivanov still couldn't quite believe what he was reading.

Nervously clearing his throat, he thoughtfully folded the signal, running his fingers backward and forwards across the crease and suggested that given Cavendish's pre-eminence, his identity would have been restricted to a designated KGB officer at their London Station.

Spencer crumpled his face in response.

Ivanov rolled his eyes in despair and threw his hands out in a pleading gesture. 'Oh, come on, we both know it's standard procedure...keep the protocols tight and protect your source at all costs! As *you* did with me!' he added, pointing his finger in a stabbing motion.

'The trouble is, Alexei, I really can't think of anyone at the Embassy Vasiliev would trust enough with running Cavendish.' He paused to take a couple of puffs on his cigarette. 'Well...at least no-one who immediately springs to mind.'

'I'd have thought it was obvious, the Head of Station,' Ivanov said, accompanied by a droll smile.

'Smolin? You can't *be* serious!'

'Never more so.'

Spencer passed him a puzzled look.

'Think about it.'

'I'm trying to.'

Ivanov started pacing the room, only pausing to serve himself a neat vodka. He was talking in fits and starts.

While he accepted Vasiliev had often been critical of Smolin's running of the KGB's London Station and had scathingly referred to him as "yesterday's man". Ivanov explained that despite Comrade Vasiliev's long-term political ambitions and sense of self-importance, the men Smolin had once fought alongside during the war still held sway behind the imposing red-bricked walls of the Kremlin. Ivanov suggested with some reason it would take a brave man to make a move against Smolin without risking the wrath of the old guard in Moscow.

After earning his spurs and reputation during

the siege of Stalingrad, Smolin had been awarded the "Order of Victory" by Stalin. It was the ultimate accolade. As a renowned Soviet war hero, at home, he still commanded enormous respect.

The siege had been one of the bloodiest and most crucial battles of World War II, eventually ending in the catastrophic defeat of Hitler's increasingly beleaguered invading army. From August 1941 to February 1943, more than two million troops had fought in close quarters. Civilian casualties were still largely unknown; even the most conservative estimates ran into the tens of thousands.

Ivanov took a large slug of vodka. 'You have to believe me, Sir Spencer, if I'd known Bradley was about to be killed, I'd have warned him off!' he pleaded passionately.

Spencer still felt a deep-rooted sense of guilt over his death. Assigning him to Ivanov was, in many respects, a calculated risk, but it was one Bradley was eventually willing to take.

At the time, Joyce had openly questioned Spencer's decision, suggesting he was playing with fire, that Bradley was way too inexperienced to take on their prized Soviet agent and would end up screwing the entire operation. She had had a point, but relative novice or not, there was far more to the seemingly superficially engaging, socially slick, wealthy playboy. Bradley also possessed surprising integrity and was far deeper and more complicated than even Spencer had initially expected.

Admittedly, things had not always gone entirely smoothly. Spencer recalled having received a report from Bradley's somewhat stressed instructors during his basic training; it evoked a wry smile. By all accounts, Bradley's performance on the firing ranges had proved to have been particularly hair-raising.

Dubious firearm skills aside, Bradley had exceeded all expectations and had played an absolute blinder in skilfully helping to cultivate Ivanov, where far more seasoned officers had failed in the past to persuade him to commit fully. British Intelligence owed Bradley a considerable debt. The only downside to Bradley's success was that unlike more experienced field officers, Spencer was all too aware that he would never have stood a fighting chance against a highly skilled professional KGB assassin.

Ivanov's voice broke through his thoughts. 'You have to believe me, the last thing I ever wanted was to have Bradley's blood on my hands!'

Spencer took his time weighing up his reply. 'Well, I'd certainly like to think so, Alexei, but then again, I suppose that all rather depends on whether or not we're singing off the same hymn sheet.'

'Bradley was a *good* man,' Ivanov answered emotionally. 'Loyal, kind…I trusted him with my life!'

'Yes, I have a feeling you might have done,' came the non-committal response.

'Do you think there's a possibility he was onto Cavendish?'

Spencer shrugged. 'Well, I can't think of any other reason why Vasiliev would risk ordering his execution. I've no proof, of course, and maybe we never will.'

Ivanov frowned before momentarily turning his head away from Spencer's scrutiny. He was struggling with his emotions. 'I suppose,' he said at length, 'only time will prove my innocence, that, in some ways, I'm just as much a victim of your Agent Wolf as Bradley ever was!'

'Perhaps you're right,' Spencer said, moving over to the hearth and pressing the brass bell beside it.

Ivanov came to his feet, ramrod straight, hands clasped tightly behind his back. 'Is my family still in Moscow?' he asked anxiously.

'Yes, they are.'

'At our flat?'

Spencer confirmed they were.

'You'll keep the Canadians informed of their whereabouts?'

'You have my word.'

'Thank you,' Ivanov whispered.

In response to Spencer's summons came the sound of footsteps approaching on the creaking hallway floorboards. Ivanov's gaze worked uneasily toward the oak-panelled door. Lewis was the first to enter, followed closely by Joyce.

'Are you all set to leave?' Spencer asked Lewis.

'Yes, sir, we are.'

Spencer turned back to face Ivanov. Behind the Russian's slight smile, he was nervous. 'I hope one day we'll be able to meet under somewhat better circumstances,' he said, extending his hand.

'So do I, Sir Spencer...so, *do I!*'

CHAPTER 26

Southwater Estate
West Sussex

With the meeting at an end, Spencer eased on his pinstripe jacket, his gaze drifting thoughtfully toward the large sash windows. A sharp downpour was once again lashing heavily against the glass panes. He imagined Jock Weir was probably anxious to get going before the weather took a turn for the worse. Before taking off from RAF Northolt, the Met Office forecast had predicted increasingly blustery conditions heading in from the southwest, with torrential rain overnight. A less experienced pilot might well have called it a day, but knowing the Weir of old, he'd be confident enough to press on.

Hearing the phone ring, Spencer walked over to the sideboard. 'DG here,' he answered sharply.

There was a slight hesitation at the end of the

line; he had obviously taken them by surprise. 'It's Oscar 1 here, sir.' His voice sounded tense. Tim Colgate was an experienced MI5 field officer and headed up the estate's security detail.

'Go ahead.'

'Abort flight now; we have a contact, heavily armed!'

'Egorov's team?'

'Yes, sir.'

There was a beat of silence between them. '*I was assured* you had the entire estate on lockdown.' Spencer waited for a response. 'Oscar 1, are you still there?' he pressed, irritation creeping into his voice.

'I thought we had, sir,' came the tense response.

'We'll talk later...sort it!' Spencer rasped, slamming the receiver down on him.

Following the attack on Ivanov's convoy, with two men down, depleted or not, the former *Spetsnaz* team's second-in-command, Peter Galin, was still out there and came with a ruthless reputation, as did his compatriot, Sergey Yudin. They'd have undoubtedly gone to ground and re-grouped, considered their options, but, more importantly, would have awaited further instructions from Moscow Central.

Although Vasiliev's team had been temporarily placed on the backfoot, Spencer always suspected it unlikely Moscow Central would decide to pull the plug on their assignment. There again, why would they? In Vasiliev's shoes, he'd undoubtedly have chanced his arm and gone for broke. The Soviet's intelligence continued to be spot on. The ripple effect of Cavendish's treachery was still obviously paying dividends to his KGB masters.

Taking Cavendish out of the equation was all well and good. Still, Spencer feared the ripple effect of his treachery, and the KGB's infiltration of the Service's overseas arm was already so deep-rooted, that British Intelligence was still leaking like a veritable sieve, with those still blindly loyal to their disgraced former boss. They probably continued to view him as nothing less than a political martyr to their communist cause.

In many ways, Spencer blamed himself, that he'd somehow been fooled and entirely hoodwinked by someone whom he'd once trusted implicitly.

As Spencer scooped up his briefcase and turned toward the window, there was a blinding flash, followed by a piercing, ear-splitting, gut-wrenching explosion as Weir's tiny four-seater plane was blown wide apart. There was a sudden bright light accompanied by a ball of fire. Swiftly followed by a pall of choking, black billowing smoke as jagged chunks of metal slammed into the house and ricocheted across the rain-sodden lawns creating huge divots of grass and soil.

Everything was in slow-motion as the sheer force of the resulting shockwave not only sucked Spencer's breath away, but knocked him clean off his feet as he was sent spiralling helplessly across the room before landing awkwardly against a bookcase. The heavy leather-bound tomes crashed down on top of him as ragged chunks of the ceiling plaster and lethal shards of glass imploded from the sash windows.

⊨+ +⊨

Outside the mansion, the mangled wreck of the plane was engulfed in flames and a pall of black billowing smoke. Galin's KGB compatriot, Yudin, had sprayed the fuselage of the aircraft with an automatic sub-machine, igniting the fuel tank and the nearby tender which had just finished refuelling the plane for the return journey to RAF Northwood.

Although Oscar 1's warning had probably saved their lives by ordering them back inside, away from the plane, they were still far from out of danger. They had only just managed to return to the hallway, when the explosion tore through the mansion, sending Lewis spiralling helplessly across the black and white tiled hall before thudding heavily against a wall. Winded and in pain, he lay for a moment tucked up in a defensive foetal position.

The explosion was followed simultaneously by an ear-splitting, deafening emergency alarm erupting throughout the entire building. The shrill piercing noise from the alarm was almost unbearable.

Above the pulsating alarm, Lewis could vaguely make out Joyce letting out an endless stream of expletives. Interwoven with hacking coughs as she desperately tried to clear her lungs of clogging dust. *Thank god, she's still alive!* he found himself thinking.

'Jo…Jo, are you okay?' he gasped, calling out to her.

'I've no bloody idea!' she choked, to the point of retching.

Although the force of the blast had propelled her away from the front door, and she only narrowly missed being crushed under the weight of the enormous chandelier sent hurtling down from the ceiling. Either way, she was lucky to be alive.

'Where the hell's Ivanov, can you see him?' Lewis snorted through the fugue of smoke and debris.

Easing himself forward, Lewis's gaze wandered fleetingly toward the once impressive and supposedly re-enforced double doors hanging helplessly off their hinges. Then again, if they hadn't been reinforced, it was doubtful if any of them would have survived the blast. Outside the mansion, Jock Weir's plane was still burning fiercely, and he could hear what sounded like intermittent bursts of gunfire and the screaming from their colleagues who had survived the blast. *But where the hell was Carter? Did he make it?*

Lewis turned sharply; Joyce was yelling at him for help. With the dust slowly beginning to settle, he could just make our she had a tight grip of Ivanov's arm. She was practically hauling to him to his feet.

'Come on, Alexei, move, move!'

'I can't,' he pleaded, wheezily gasping for breath.

'I'm sorry, Alexei, we don't have a bloody choice!' she said, propelling him across the hallway.

Lewis scrambled to his feet and hurriedly fell in beside them, taking hold of Ivanov's other arm as they crunched their way through the broken shards of glass and debris littering the floor.

Ivanov was bleeding heavily from a gash to his mouth. 'Where are…'

Joyce cut in. 'You know the drill, to the safe room!'

Crisscrossing beneath the sprawling mansion was a myriad of almost identical corridors. Shortly after their arrival, Oscar 1 had put them through a daily exercise to familiarise themselves with the way to the safe room. At first, it had proved almost as confusing to Ivanov as his MI5 minders. However, after two weeks of constant practice, with mutual agreement, they reached a point where even Ivanov felt comfortable that he could have found his way there practically blindfolded.

The safe room was installed behind what appeared to be an unprepossessing wooden panelled door. Outwardly, it looked no different from any of the other rooms leading off from the corridor. However, its dark oak veneer disguised a bank vault styled steel door and matching frame with a heavy-duty deadlock.

The spartan reinforced room was designed to hold a maximum of eight people, with ten square feet of floor space per person. The as yet untested design was meant to provide sufficient air for up to five hours before a potentially dangerous build-up of carbon dioxide occurred. It was starkly furnished, containing a small toilet cubicle, along with a fresh water supply, food, and a basic medical supply. Crucially, the room bristled with communication equipment, with direct links to the estate's security team, and also to the Ops Commanders of both MI5 and Special Branch. Sited immediately to the right of the heavily reinforced door was a large weapons rack, bristling with an array of armoury including hand grenades.

Although Ivanov had always found the windowless room claustrophobic, he knew full well his life might one day, as now, depend on reaching it. Even so, for a man of his age, it was no easy task, even at the best of times.

They steered him out of the hallway and along the corridor toward the staircase leading down to the safe room, Ivanov was already struggling. His chest was heaving and drenched in sweat. The veins in his neck were seemingly about to burst.

He stumbled slightly. They steadied him, paused a moment before continuing. Lewis held Joyce's eyes for a second; his expression said it all. At this rate, there was every chance he'd drop dead long before they reached the safe room.

'Alexei, are you going to be okay?' she asked, her voice etched with concern.

Ivanov couldn't quite summon enough breath to

answer, but managed a slight smile and inclined his head.

Joyce glanced across at Lewis, who screwed up his face uneasily.

'Alexei,' she pressed, 'are you sure about this?'

Ivanov nodded, determined to make it down to the safe room. He was fuelled by adrenaline and a deep-rooted instinct for survival. With their increasing support, intermingled with his loud rasps, he somehow managed to keep moving along the dimly lit corridor.

As they neared the staircase leading down to the bowels of the building, Joyce slipped her arm out of Ivanov's and headed over to a large metal framed ottoman styled box. She opened the brass catch and flipped opened the lid. Joyce raided the box and slipped a Browning 9mm pistol into the waistband of her skirt, before retrieving two Sterling submachine guns. She paused slightly; someone had thankfully killed the emergency alarm.

'Here take this,' she said, handing one of them to Lewis.

As Joyce swung round to take hold of Ivanov's arm, catching a rapid movement out of the corner of her eye, she half-turned and automatically checking with her thumb that she'd released the safety catch, and at the same time immediately raised the Sterling. But was a fraction too late.

At the same time, in one swift movement, the figure of a tall, lean man emerged at the end of the corridor and fired off a single shot. Joyce squeezed the Sterling's trigger and let rip with a short, sharp burst as he retreated around the corner. She looked over her shoulder to see Ivanov had collapsed to the floor and doubled over in pain.

'*Stay* with him!' she ordered Lewis.

His first instinct was to protect her back, but there was no point arguing.

The fact he had fired off a single round meant he was trying to conserve his ammunition.

Carefully edging her way along the corridor, another single shot rang out. Taking a gulp of air, Joyce gingerly peered around the corner. Lying dead on the floor was a member of the estate's security team. Stooping to retrieve his weapon, was the same tall, cropped haired figure, wearing black stove-piped jeans and matching casual open-necked shirt, who had shot Ivanov. She now knew for sure he was running out of ammunition and had the upper hand. Joyce held back a little and instantly recognised his distinctive Slavic features from the Russian Embassy surveillance photos. It was Peter Galin, the *Spetsnaz* team's second-in-command.

With the Sterling raised, she stepped out. 'Move a muscle, Comrade, and I'll drop you where you stand!'

Although Galin didn't appear to flinch a muscle, he *was* taken aback by being addressed in Russian, and especially by a woman. She wasn't quite fluent, but it was near enough. Galin weighed up his options. He really didn't have that many.

She repeated the command. For some reason, Galin had a distinct feeling this MI5 officer wouldn't hesitate to carry out her threat and drop him on the spot, and slowly released grip of his Makarov and her colleague's Browning pistol.

As they noisily clattered to the stone floor, Galin stiffened and slowly turned to face her.

'Get your hands in the air, Comrade!'

'Your Russian is excellent,' Galvin ventured, playing for time as he stared down the barrel of the Sterling,

'Get down!' Joyce gestured, pointing the automatic toward the floor.

Galin hesitated a fraction before dropping to his knees.

'Spread eagle *now!*'

'And what if I don't?' Galin ventured.

'I think we both know the answer to that.'

Galin toyed with the idea of surrender. He was the last man standing. After destroying the plane, Yudin lay dead in a nearby copse following a short exchange of gunfire. Abandoning all caution, his bravery had allowed him just enough cover to reach the mansion.

It was a stark choice between life or death. Galin desperately wanted to live, to give up. But, if he were captured alive, there would be no forgiveness in Moscow. At least this way his family would be cared for, and wouldn't suffer the humiliation and shame of surrender.

No, Galin decided, for the sake of his family and the honour of his fallen Comrades, his only choice was to go down fighting.

Galin briefly closed his eyes. *Make it clean, make it quick,* he said silently to Joyce before reaching inside his shirt to withdraw a handgun from a concealed chamois holster.

Without the slightest hesitation, Joyce closed her right index finger around the trigger and let off a short, sharp burst of the Sterling. She'd answered his silent prayer. Galin was dead before he hit the ground.

Walking past his lifeless body, she barely gave him a second glance. Placing the Sterling latterly in her arm, Joyce retraced her way back along the corridor to find Lewis crouched over Ivanov. He looked up and shook his head.

CHAPTER 27

Southwater Estate
West Sussex

'Spence, for god's sake, are you, all right?' Joyce said, anxiously kneeling down beside him. *God, please don't let him die on me, please!*

Her voice slow pierced his consciousness. For some reason, the world seemed strangely detached as a sudden wave of sickness swept over him. Her voice sounded distant as if she was calling his name in a dark echoing tunnel.

Spencer's eyes felt so heavy it was almost as if they had been zipped tight shut. Forcing them open, the sudden influx of light was blinding and blinked several times. Through the grey misty haze, at first, he could just about make out a half shape as she bent over him.

Joyce called his name again; her voice was an odd

mix of fear, coupled with anger. 'Don't *you* bloody well go dying on me, Spence!'

Feeling her gently stroke his cheek, he instinctively reached out in search of her hand, but couldn't fathom why it felt like he had a huge weight on him. He blinked a couple of times, suddenly aware something wet and warm was streaming down his face; he was bleeding heavily from a large gash to his forehead. The strange part was, he didn't yet feel any pain, but from bitter experience, he knew that once the adrenaline rush subsided, the pain would kick in with a vengeance.

Joyce hurriedly removed her silk neck scarf and pressed it firmly against the wound in an attempt to stem the bleeding.

Noticing the fear on her face, he whispered gently, 'Don't worry, Jo, I'm not going to die on you.'

'You'd better ruddy not!' She smiled down at him, eyes swimming with tears.

'Did Weir make it?'

'The poor sod didn't stand a chance.'

'And Ivanov?'

Joyce missed a slight beat before reluctantly admitting Galin had taken him out.

'Dead?' Spencer repeated quietly.

She found herself mumbling an apology of sorts, that Ivanov had died on her watch.

'Help me up!' he demanded. 'Is Galin still on the loose?'

'I shot him,' she said matter-of-factly. 'And you're

not going anywhere; you'll kill yourself! I'd better tell you sooner, rather than later, but Carter's been injured.'

'Badly?

'He's a bit messed up, but he'll live.'

'What about Yudin?'

'You'll have to ask Oscar 1; I've no idea.'

Joyce squeezed his hand lightly. For once in his life, he wasn't prepared to fight her.

Spencer was feeling far weaker than he was willing to admit. He stared up at her eyes and noticed a piece of white plaster entangled in her hair, and smudges of dirt blackened her stunning face. 'Are *you* okay?'

Joyce wrinkled her nose, but wouldn't be drawn and turned sharply. She glanced over her shoulder to see Tim Colgate, Oscar 1, the head of the estate's security, accompanied by two heavily armed officers framed in the doorway. Seeing Spencer stricken on the floor, he paused slightly before addressing Joyce.

'We need to move, ma'am; I've called a Blue Alert!'

Joyce thanked him. She would have been disappointed if he hadn't.

The alert required an immediate response from both MI5 and Special Branch officers. Backup assets would be deployed from London and their respective outstations across the Home Counties surrounding the estate. Once a Blue Alert was in force, protocol demanded the Director-General be whisked away from the scene and out of harm's way. In this case, it was a little too late in the day, but they still needed to move him as fast as reasonably possible to the nearest secure military hospital.

Spencer's grip suddenly tightened vice-like around her hand.

She looked down at him and smiled knowingly before asking Colgate to give them a minute by themselves. They dutifully backed off into the hallway and waited until ordered to return.

Once they were alone, Spencer awkwardly propped himself up on his elbow. 'Over the last few weeks, Vasiliev's people have been handed everything on a plate by one of us! They've successfully shadowed our every move; every plan from St Barnabas Mews to the estate has been passed to Moscow Central.'

Joyce looked down at him curiously. 'But surely this isn't down to Cavendish,' she parried. 'He's under house arrest. There's no way…'

'House arrest or not, Jo, we both damn well know Cavendish is at the heart of a cabal of disaffected, like-minded MI6 traitors, and whether we like it or not, they're still leaking like a bloody sieve to their communist puppet masters.'

Gingerly removing the scarf from his forehead, Joyce wearily sat back on her haunches. The bleeding had finally reduced to little more than a trickle. Although Spencer was trying to fight it, she was concerned by just how much blood he had already lost.

'Here, take it,' she said, handing over the stained silk scarf.

He thanked her.

'So, what do we do now?' she said, barely above a whisper.

'I'd have thought it was obvious.'

She held his eyes steadily. 'I don't know, is it? You tell me.'

'Come on, Jo, do I really have to spell it out to you?'

Joyce slowly, thoughtfully sucked in her lower lip and said tentatively, 'I reckon you'll have to.'

Spencer made it clear that, as far as he was concerned, Cavendish was little more than a waste of space and oxygen. Too many good people had already died because of his treachery. It was time to draw a line under his power and reach, once and for all.

'Do you get *my* drift?' he added, in his customary silky, yet deceptively chilling voice.

Joyce took a fraction before reluctantly nodding in response. She'd got his drift alright, but it was still one hell of an ask, to take down someone of Cavendish's stature.

'Jesus wept, Spence, I'm really not sure I can do it,' she murmured.

'Just play it carefully, Jo,' he said with a distinct harshness.

A faint, somewhat resigned smile began hovering on her lips. 'Well…if I don't, then I guess, one way or another, we're probably all bloody screwed!'

CHAPTER 28

Chowles House
Surrey

By the time Garvan arrived at the pleasant, white stuccoed house, it was almost 3 pm. On the surface, at least, it was merely a tragic case of a former top-ranking civil servant ending their own life.

His chauffeur-driven Wolseley was stopped for a brief security check before being waved through the extensive local police cordon and directed toward the house, where they greeted by the senior officer in charge, Detective Chief Inspector Scott Armstrong.

Aware the deceased had regularly entertained the Foreign Secretary, which had required a low-key police presence from nearby Guildford, Armstrong had decided to place what he'd thought to be a routine call through to Scotland Yard's Special

Branch informing them of the sudden death of the Foreign Secretary's friend, and presumably ex-colleague.

However, on recognising the tall, familiar figure of the Assistant Commissioner alight from the rear of the official car, he realised the deceased, Sir Dick Cavendish, probably wasn't quite the grey Whitehall mandarin he had always assumed. Top brass didn't move a muscle unless it was important.

Armstrong's expression didn't falter and hoped he'd covered his surprise well. He extended his hand in welcome to his former and occasionally irascible boss.

Garvan returned the younger man's smile. 'It's been a long time, Scott.'

'Yes, I suppose it has, Guv,' came the slightly awkward response.

Their paths had first crossed at the Met long before his eventual transfer on promotion to the Surrey Constabulary. At the Yard, Armstrong had been viewed as a gifted detective, but after a year serving with Special Branch under Garvan's command, it was felt the competition was perhaps way too fierce for him to make the grade.

Armstrong could quite easily have returned to the CID and resumed his already successful career with West End Central's murder squad. To save face, and fearing there would always be a certain stigma attached to his failure, he had requested an immediate transfer outside of the Met. At the time, it had been a bitter pill to swallow and, even now, still rankled deeply with him.

Finding himself confronted by his former boss, he dug deep, trying not to allow his old insecurities to resurface…that he wasn't quite talented enough for Special Branch.

Sensing Armstrong's unease, Garvan calmly took his time surveying the house before joking, 'I don't know about you, Scott, but I reckon we're obviously in the wrong game.'

'That's for sure!' he responded with the merest flicker of a smile, before leading the way toward a seemingly unobtrusive side-gate.

Much to Garvan's surprise, it opened out onto a spacious garden and large swimming pool, with its pristine blue surface glistening in the afternoon sunlight. The pool was surrounded by attractive sandstone flagging and flanked either side with neatly striped deckchairs interspersed by small circular tables. The garden was an eclectic mix of sculptured privet hedges, well-established shrubbery, and immaculately kept lawns.

Garvan knew that Cavendish's rather well-heeled lifestyle and spending power had little if anything to do with his career as a "civil servant". He'd married into money, but still hadn't quite expected the family pile to be on such a grand scale.

If the reports were to be believed, Cavendish had never wanted or desired payment from his Soviet spymasters, well, that is, other than the occasional bottle of vodka, but then again, with his wife's deep pockets, he didn't exactly need the money.

After graduating from Cambridge, whether by design or not, Cavendish had made a rather astute move by marrying Jenny Campbell, the daughter of a city banker with paternal connections to the Duke of Argyll. By all accounts, it was a love match. Garvan's personal views about their relationship were somewhat more cynical. Whether Cavendish had deliberately targeted Jenny or not, Cavendish's newfound wealth and aristocratic family connections appeared not to have diminished his communist idealism one iota, nor his blinkered, obsessive crusade against the supposed evils of Western capitalism.

Armstrong led him over to Cavendish's body. He was slumped back in one of the deckchairs; his mouth was wide open as if gasping for his last breath of air. He was dressed casually in a white, opened necked shirt, with the sleeves neatly rolled back to the elbows. A Panama hat was neatly resting on his lap, poking out from underneath was an unopened paperback. Garvan asked whether or not the doctor had mentioned how long he might have been dead.

'No, Guv, not yet.'

Judging by Cavendish's grey waxy pallor, it was likely to have been quite some considerable time.

Garvan's gaze roamed thoughtfully away from the body toward a broken glass tumbler lying beside the deckchair and a pair of gold-framed sunglasses.

There was an opened brown bottle of codeine tablets near his right foot; its top had either rolled or fallen to the edge of the swimming pool.

His attention slowly drifted toward the circular wooden table beside Cavendish's deckchair. On it sat a rather expensive looking, monogrammed leather-bound metallic hip flask. It briefly crossed Garvan's mind that he really wouldn't mind having one for himself. When off-duty, he loved nothing more than relaxing beside a fishing lake, alone with his thoughts, feeling and hearing the breeze rustling through the trees, interspersed with the occasional exhilaration of catching a fish and taking the odd tipple from a flask.

Noticing Garvan's interest, Armstrong said it appeared to contain the remnants of a clear alcoholic spirit.

'Vodka?' Garvan queried, with a faint smile.

'To be honest with you, Guv, we're not entirely sure. We'll have to wait for the lab tests to come back.'

'Yes...yes, of course,' he said distractedly.

For some reason, the doctor looked vaguely familiar. Throughout his career, Garvan had, as yet, never met a pathologist he hadn't either respected or admired. In his experience, they were a complete breed apart—detectives in their own right. Their professionalism in helping the police to solve either unexplained or sudden deaths often provided a much-needed voice for murder victims, ensuring their killers would eventually be convicted and brought to justice.

The pathologist's smartly dressed female assistant struck Garvan as surprisingly young for what he'd always viewed as a particularly gruesome choice of career. During his time, he'd certainly experienced his fair share of some pretty horrific sights, but fortunately rarely on a daily basis. Try as he might, Garvan had never yet quite managed to attend a post-mortem without feeling slightly queasy.

'How long have they been here?' he asked Armstrong.

'Well, not really too long. The local police surgeon was the first on the scene. After pronouncing Cavendish officially dead, he called in Dr Tait straightaway to take over.'

'I can't help thinking that I've met him somewhere before.'

'You may well have, Guv; he used to work out of West End Central.'

'That might explain it, then,' Garvan said thoughtfully.

'Back in December, Tait transferred down to Surrey after a stint in the north of England.'

'Who found the body?'

'Jenny Cavendish.'

Garvan remained poker-faced but was surprised.

After alerting the police, Armstrong explained, the first officer on the scene was the village PC, who quickly realised he needed backup from CID. By all accounts, Cavendish's wife had been staying with their daughter, Marie, and her family in London. Although she wasn't due to return home until the weekend, she'd become increasingly concerned after speaking to her husband last night.

'Why?'

'He seemed depressed...more so than before.'

'So why didn't she return home there and then?'

'Cavendish apparently asked her not to.'

Garvan looked at him questioningly.

'It was their grandson's birthday; he didn't apparently want to go spoiling things for them.'

After her husband's recent retirement from the "civil service", Jenny had told Armstrong that he had become increasingly moody and withdrawn. At first, she'd simply put it down to the fact he was having difficulty adjusting to kicking his heels at home and missing the routine of being at work. However, things had seemingly come to a head after he unexpectedly announced he was cancelling the membership of his golf club. Up until then, it had been the one great love of his life, a real passion.

At that point, Jenny confessed, she knew something was seriously wrong, but she couldn't get through to him. He kept stonewalling her and refused to be drawn, although had recently complained of feeling unwell, it was nothing too serious, just a stomach upset. Even so, it was only at her husband's insistence she left for London to stay with their daughter and three-year-old grandson, Jamie.

Last night on the phone, he had seemed even more distant than before, so Jenny had decided to cut short her visit and caught the first available train out of Waterloo Station to Guildford. After catching a taxi, she had arrived home a little before 7.30 am. Having searched the house for her husband, she had eventually discovered his body slumped in the deckchair beside the swimming pool.

On face value, it all seemed entirely plausible. Why wouldn't Armstrong buy it? But Lady Cavendish wasn't quite the innocent grieving widow she appeared to be. Jenny knew how to play the game and was every bit as astute, if not more so, than her late husband.

Given everything that was going on in her husband's life, Garvan would have been slightly more surprised if Cavendish hadn't only felt down but possibly even suicidal.

Jenny certainly wasn't quite all she seemed. Beneath the heartfelt tears, the desolate grieving widow was not only aware of her late husband's double life as a Soviet agent, but had reportedly shared many of his more extreme far-left political leanings. However, complicit Jenny may or may not have been in her husband's dual role as a Soviet agent was still very much an ongoing investigation.

In spite of their ardent communist idealism and manifest hatred of Western capitalism and all it stood for, the Cavendishs certainly hadn't ever considered giving up the finer things in life and had wasted little time in ensuring their daughter's substantial inheritance was ring-fenced beyond the reaches of the UK Tax Office.

Garvan assumed Jenny's reticence in cooperating fully with Armstrong was no doubt driven by an amalgam of fear, self-preservation, and an overwhelming desire to protect the family and her husband's secrets from the public domain. But given Jenny's situation, he couldn't understand why on earth she had supposedly involved the local police, or quite why MI5 had allowed her to contact them in the first place.

After Dick Cavendish's enforced "retirement" from the Service, by default, Jenny had also found herself under house arrest in all but name, with a succession of senior MI5 officers turning up on their doorstep to interrogate both Jenny and her disgraced husband.

Her trip to London would have needed MI5's approval. Garvan somehow doubted she'd have been allowed to travel alone. If, as Jenny told Armstrong, she'd called her husband the night before he supposedly killed himself, their conversation would undoubtedly have been recorded…that's if it had ever happened at all.

Of slightly more interest to Garvan was why Spencer had decided to withdraw his officers from Chowles House. Officially, it was still on lockdown. So quite how Dick Cavendish committed suicide without MI5 knowing was stretching his imagination more than just a little.

At least perhaps it went some way in explaining why he hadn't yet managed to speak with Spencer. On learning of Cavendish's death, he had immediately tried contacting him at the Cambridge Military Hospital in Aldershot, where he was still recovering from his injuries sustained at the estate. Even so, they remained in regular contact, and it was unusual not to have heard back from him by now.

Garvan had wanted to run things by him before approaching Whitehall. As MI6's former Chief, his unexpected and as yet unexplained death was potentially a matter of national importance. Garvan had wanted to be sure of his ground before informing the PM and the Home and Foreign secretaries with news of Cavendish's demise.

Failing to receive an answer, Garvan had decided to contact Dawn Abrams at the office. She'd apologised and wasn't quite sure why Spencer hadn't returned his call, but promised they would get back to him.

Garvan had thanked her, but knew when he was being fobbed off. God only knew what Spencer was up to. Given the enormity of Cavendish's apparent suicide, he had fully expected to hear back from him on the car phone. Garvan could only surmise that something had either gone drastically wrong or, as he feared, his old friend was playing a double-edged sword.

According to Armstrong, although the grieving widow was understandably distraught, for some inexplicable reason, she seemed markedly reluctant to discuss her husband in any great detail, almost to the point of being deliberately obstructive.

When asked whether he had remained in touch with any of his former work colleagues, to what had seemed like a reasonably innocuous enquiry was met by a surprising and, he guessed, contrived vagueness. When pressed further, Jenny admitted there had been one or two, but who they were; she'd really no idea. It hadn't particularly interested her.

Jenny told him they had always lived a relatively solitary life. There was the occasional whist evening at the village hall, and in his younger days, Dick had enjoyed playing cricket with the local team. In later years, he had taken up golf, which had swiftly proved to be an abiding passion. Apart from his forays to the clubhouse, by and large, they still preferred to keep themselves to themselves and were more than happy in their own company. They rarely entertained, and then only with a small select circle of close friends.

When Armstrong pressed Jenny whether that had included the Foreign Secretary, judging by her suddenly sour demeanour, it was something of a sore point, and at first, she seemed more than a little reluctant to be drawn. But eventually, she decided she had little choice other than confess he had been a family friend for many years.

Armstrong knew damn well she was hiding something from him, but what was it, and why? He couldn't quite fathom it out and looked to Garvan as if for help, but none was forthcoming.

By now, his former boss was rather more intent on watching Dr Tait take a studied step back from the body and nod almost as if to himself, before whipping off his horn-rimmed glasses and looked expectantly to the police photographer.

'That's it. I have the whole body, Doc.'

'And the close-ups?'

'Everything.'

'Then I think it's probably about time we started calling it a day,' he said, addressing his assistant, Ellie.

She glanced up from her notepad.

'Do you have everything we need?' Tait queried.

Ellie took a moment scanning her notes, before snapping the cover shut. 'Yes, sir, we do,' she answered emphatically. 'And what about the photos?'

'If you're happy, Ellie, then so am I.' He smiled reassuringly.

Tait had been so engrossed in his preliminary examination of Cavendish's body; he hadn't noticed that he was being observed. He smiled briefly at Armstrong before thoughtfully turning his attention toward Garvan, his eyes narrowing questioningly.

'Haven't we met somewhere before?'

'I was thinking much the same thing. Maybe it's an age thing, but for the life of me, I can't quite remember where…or when for that matter.'

Tait sucked in his lower lip before suddenly

clicking his fingers, shaking his head, grimacing in disgust. 'I've got it, it was the Bramley case, wasn't it!'

Digging deep, Garvan owned up; he was right. Over the years, Tait hadn't aged particularly well. The last time he had seen him was back in the war, when the newly qualified pathologist had sported a mop of closely cropped dark curly hair. Sadly, the once luxuriant curls had long gone, as had most of his hair.

There was a large part of Garvan that wished Tait hadn't reminded him of the tragic murder enquiry. Long before joining the ranks of Special Branch, he had already earned his spurs as a successful CID detective. Rosie Bramley had just started school and, during her very first half-term break, went missing on a trip to the local sweet shop at the end of the street where she lived. A week after her disappearance, the poor child's partially clothed body was discovered by workmen buried beneath the rubble of a World War II bomb site. It had been a particularly brutal murder, and one that had haunted Garvan ever since.

It had always been drummed into Garvan that feelings have no place in a murder enquiry. In the main, he was inclined to agree; however, he had struggled to overcome his gut instincts and moral repulsion, but the mere mention of the child's name brought back his revulsion and feelings of utter disgust toward her killer.

But long before joining the police, Garvan had always been adroit at managing his emotions, keeping them buried rather than experiencing them. Since his mother's death at a young age, he now suspected this was nothing more than a coping mechanism to suppress in his young mind, the overwhelming sadness and anxiety caused by her sudden death.

His desolate father had tried to fill the void, but he'd grown up in a household filled with awkward silences and lack of emotion; it was, for the most part, a sad, empty upbringing. Even now, his mother's death cast a huge shadow over his life. Perhaps, in hindsight, it explained how he had occasionally felt emotionally out of his depth with Joyce. There were times when she'd wanted more from him. And she was right. He'd always found himself fighting not only to gain her trust, but also her affection.

As Tait toyed with his glasses, his soft voice cut through Garvan's thoughts. 'At least we got there in the end.'

'Did we?' he answered uneasily.

'Yes, I think we did.'

Garvan still looked sceptical.

'I'm rarely an advocate for capital punishment,' Tait continued, 'but with the Bramley case...well, it somehow seemed rather fitting.'

Garvan inclined his head silently in agreement.

'I understand you've done quite well for yourself.' Tait smiled crookedly at him.

Garvan smiled in return. 'I'm certainly not complaining.'

Tait half-turned, gesturing toward Cavendish's body. 'We're about all done here. I've decided not to take a rectal temperature until we get back to the morgue. As he's fully clothed, I didn't want to run the risk of upsetting *your* forensic people by removing them,' he said to Armstrong.

'No…no, of course not, sir, but I assumed it was a straightforward suicide.'

'I'm not saying it isn't, Chief Inspector; I'm merely stating a fact. We need to have his body removed to the mortuary as soon as reasonably possible to ascertain his body temperature.'

Armstrong nodded sagely. 'How long do you think he's been dead, Doc?'

Other than suggesting life had expired within the last twenty-four hours, Tait was reluctant to commit himself.

'Can't you tell from the rigor mortis?'

'Well, as you can see, he's certainly been dead a while, but it's not that easy to determine. Why not ask the Assistant Commissioner? I'm sure he'll confirm it depends on many variables, outside temperature, and so on. Rest assured, I'll be in touch after the post-mortem. But, as I'm sure you're already aware, the toxicology results will take a few weeks to come through,' Tait continued, toying with his glasses. 'I take it you'll pass a copy of my report to the Assistant Commissioner?'

'Yes, sir, of course.'

'Good, then I'll be getting off. Will I see you in the post-mortem room, Chief Inspector?'

Armstrong reluctantly said that he would. He hadn't attended one in quite a while and, up until Garvan's arrival on the scene, had decided to palm it off to one of his junior colleagues. Armstrong inwardly winced at the thought. He'd have to get used to it all over again, hopefully, without turning green.

Tait nodded before reaching out to shake Garvan's hand. 'I should imagine the Bramley case probably helped seal your reputation at the Yard.'

'Well, to be perfectly honest with you, I rather wish it hadn't...but yours too, I suppose?'

Tait let out a heartfelt sigh. 'Perhaps you're right, but it was you who ended up doing all the real donkey work bringing the poor child's killer to justice.' Tait slipped on his horn-rimmed glasses. 'After the court case, I never quite got the chance to thank you in person.' The hardened pathologist's eyes burned with tears.

'Believe me, it's entirely mutual,' Garvan replied, touched by Tait's unexpected display of emotion.

Tait smiled tightly in response before heading off through the garden, leaving his assistant to pack up their equipment.

Although Dr Tait was a quiet, shy, somewhat understated man, he was an excellent pathologist and wasn't scared to lock horns in the witness box with the defending counsel. His performance in young Rosie Bramley's trial had been nothing less than a tour-de-force.

Garvan found himself recalling having met the child's parents for the first time. The sheer, almost physical force of their grief had somehow resonated with his own long suppressed feelings of pain for the loss of his mother as a boy.

Armstrong's gaze thoughtfully followed the doctor's measured progress around the pool and asked whether or not Garvan wished to interview Jenny Cavendish.

Garvan took his time in answering. 'No, I don't think that'll be necessary. Besides, I'm sure she's already had more than enough of us for one day, don't you?'

'You're probably right, Guv,' he agreed.

'If I need to come back, then I'll give you a call.' Garvan cast one last lingering look over Cavendish's body. 'Have you sent someone to pick up their daughter?'

'Well, Guv, I was going to, but Marie arrived almost at the same time as I did.'

Garvan's face registered a flicker of surprise. 'Did she drive herself?'

'No, one of her girlfriends drove her down from London.'

'Interesting,' Garvan mused distractedly. 'What time did they leave?'

'I've no idea. I never thought to ask.'

'So, where's her husband?'

'Apparently, he's in Paris on business. From what I can gather, he's the director of some fancy city financial firm or other. They're certainly not short of a bob or two!'

Garvan passed him a long, slow look. 'What time did *you* get here?'

Armstrong crumpled up his face. 'I guess it would have been about 10.15, but certainly no later than that.'

'Then they must have put their ruddy foot down,' Garvan suggested drily.

'I'm sure they did, Guv. Didn't you see that Lotus Elan parked up on the drive?'

Garvan couldn't say as he had. He wasn't particularly into cars; as long as they had four wheels and got him from A to B, that was about the extent of his interest.

'I'd give my bloody eye teeth to own a little beauty like that!' Armstrong said wistfully. 'It must have cost a small fortune.'

'I'm sure it probably did,' Garvan responded distractedly.

'Is there anything else you'd like to see, sir?'

He shook his head before briefly glancing at his watch. 'No, I'd better be making tracks. I have a meeting with the Commissioner later this afternoon. He asked me to come down just to check things out.'

Armstrong didn't entirely buy Garvan's story, but

kept his thoughts to himself and fell in beside him as he headed back toward the garden gate.

Garvan held it open for Armstrong when he caught a sudden movement out of the corner of his eye and couldn't help doing a double-take. But there was no mistaking the tall, familiar figure of Joyce Leader emerging from the house.

Glancing sharply over his shoulder, he asked Armstrong, 'Is that Marie Cavendish's girlfriend?'

Following him through the gateway, Armstrong smiled and nodded admiringly as Joyce made her way over to the Lotus. 'Yes, Guv, she is.'

'Stay here a minute, will you?' Garvan ordered with a throwaway gesture.

As she placed her handbag into the open-topped car, Garvan called out to her. She spun round in surprise before coolly adjusting her sunglasses.

'What the hell are you doing here?' she asked sharply.

'Strange that, I might as well ask you the same question.'

Joyce's left hand tightened around the car keys, but didn't respond.

'For Christ's sake, don't tell me *you*, of all people, have been tasked to comfort the grieving family?' he smirked, his voice dripping with sarcasm.

'What do you sodding think!' came the frosty reply.

'Well, that's just it, Jo. Right now, I'm not too sure what to think.'

She pulled a face, snorting dismissively.

'It's just that I couldn't help noticing you've withdrawn *your* people from the house.'

'And your point is?'

'Why not just cut the crap and stop playing games with one another?'

'It's not my call; you'd have to ask Spencer.'

'Now, why doesn't that surprise me!'

She shrugged indifferently. 'As I said, you'll have to ask the boss.'

'Well, that's just it, Jo, he isn't returning my calls.' It was difficult keeping the irritation off his face; he didn't quite succeed. 'I don't quite get why you haven't kept everything in-house.'

She stared at him questioningly.

'Why on earth would MI5 risk the local police becoming involved?'

'If you must know, it was taken entirely out of our hands. It was Cavendish's wife who contacted them...then again, I'm sure DCI Armstrong has already briefed you about what happened.'

'Interesting.'

'Is it? I'm sure you're going to tell me why.'

'From all I've read about Jenny Cavendish, she's way to savvy to have called the local plod without MI5's permission.'

Joyce stared back at him blankly. 'Maybe she did it to embarrass us.'

Garvan began shaking his head. 'Jenny's many things, but she's not a ruddy fool. For the last few weeks, your people have been crawling all over this place like a bloody rash! Are you seriously expecting me to believe MI5 didn't know Cavendish had snuffed it until she arrived home? That you just left him out there besides the pool. For Christ's sake, Jo, you can see he's been dead for hours. He's as stiff as a ruddy board!'

'He was certainly there a while before we realised he'd killed himself, yes,' she said defensively, knowing full Garvan wasn't buying it.

'*Really*?'

'After dinner last night, Cavendish asked the duty officer if it was okay to go outside and sit by the pool for a while. We'd finished with him for the day; it was as simple as that.' She shrugged. 'We left him alone.'

'And so no-one happened to notice he was carrying a bottle of codeine and a flask of booze with him?'

'Obviously not,' Joyce said dully, with a slight shrug of her shoulders. 'He often hit the bottle after dinner.' She paused a beat before adding, 'As you can imagine, things have...have been pretty awkward here. Besides, if the old bastard wanted to drink himself to death, it wasn't *our* problem. We certainly weren't going to stop him!'

Garvan scrunched up his face. 'I have to say, Jo, that scene back there was quite impressive.'

Joyce looked at him slightly quizzically. 'You tell me, was it?'

'Well, call me cynical, but it was just a little *too* stage-managed…just a little *too* perfect for my liking,' he smiled coldly, jerking his thumb toward the garden.

As far as Joyce was concerned, Garvan's arrival at Chowles House was a complete bolt out of the blue; it certainly hadn't been factored into their planning and had placed her on the backfoot. If only Spencer had picked up his call, he could well have stymied things and have prevented him from turning up, but, in fairness, he had not wanted to muddy the waters by involving his old friend in Cavendish's *apparent suicide*. Not that Garvan would believe it for one iota; his only motive had been to protect him from any potential fallout after he had decided to liquidate Cavendish.

Garvan's voice cut through her thoughts. 'So, how long was he beside the pool before your *friends* finally realised he'd snuffed it?'

Joyce figured she was on a hiding for nothing and folded her arms. 'I guess you'll have to wait for the report.'

'Oh, come on, Jo, seriously, you're not expecting me to believe MI5 left his body out there all night, *are you?*'

'To be frank with you, Luke, I'm not expecting you to believe anything I say. You rarely have!'

Garvan's smile was slight. 'As I said, Jo, from where I'm standing, it's all just a little bit too staged…a little bit too perfect. After Bradley was murdered, MI5 called Special Branch right away to clear up *your* mess!'

'That was different.'

'Precisely my point! If the Service has nothing to hide, you'd have called us immediately.'

'Perhaps, Luke, you ought to consider you are lucky that you have been left out of the loop.'

Garvan shot her a resigned, slightly jaded grin. 'Maybe you're right.'

Joyce relaxed slightly and smiled up at him. 'At least the local plod seems happy enough.'

'I'm sure they are. But whatever happened here, Jo, Cavendish didn't take his own life.'

'Then I guess it's just as well you're not the local plod, then, isn't it!'

'I'm just not quite sure how you managed to persuade Jenny Cavendish to play along with your cock and bull story.'

'I'd have thought it was obvious. Her husband's double-life has left her in a hole, and she's still digging. As any mother would, Jenny's priority is to protect her family.'

Garvan shot her a resigned, jaded smile. 'I'm sure she does…is anything else likely to come out of the woodwork?'

'I doubt it,' Joyce said, opening the driver's door of the open-topped car.

'What about the coroner's report?'

'Tait's on the books.' She winked, easing herself into the Lotus.

'So you've got to him as well.'

She shrugged, turned on the car, and started revving up the throaty engine.

'Then I take it the post-mortem will be a whitewash?'

'And what if it is? Will you seriously lose any sleep over the old bastard? I certainly won't!' Joyce said, slamming the driver's door shut. 'Think about it, Luke, if Cavendish hadn't tipped off his Soviet masters in Moscow, your guy, Lillywhite, would still be alive and at home with his family!'

Garvan's taut expression spoke volumes. It was answer enough.

'If it hadn't been for Lillywhite, they'd have taken us all out...the entire convoy,' Joyce came back at him, releasing the MG's handbrake, her voice suddenly cracked with emotion. 'Don't get me wrong, Luke, I feel sorry for Cavendish's daughter. I'm not so sure about his wife, but at the end of the day, the bastard deserved everything that was coming to him!'

As he watched Joyce speed off across gravel driveway and through the police cordon. Reluctantly, Garvan knew she probably had a point. In comparison to the murder of little Rosie Bramley, no, he was unlikely to lose any sleep over Dick Cavendish's apparent *suicide*.

CHAPTER 29

The Cambridge Military Hospital
Aldershot, Hampshire

By the time Joyce arrived at the large sprawling Victorian built hospital with its grand central block and impressive clock tower, the sky was a leaden, gunmetal grey, covered with a fine mist of rain, driven by a biting westerly wind, sweeping in waves across the carpark.

As instructed, she checked in at the main reception desk before following the signage up a darkly lit staircase leading to the first floor, where Spencer had been allocated a senior officers' side room. The long high echoing corridors were filled with the all-pervading smell of carbolic disinfectant.

Having been pre-warned by the reception clerk, the slender, smartly uniformed, no-nonsense matron, Tessa Ellis, was awaiting her arrival at the ward's nursing office and was, Joyce believed, under the impression that Spencer was some General, or other, from the War Office in Whitehall. In Matron's world, senior officers were nothing more than two a penny; they were patients and no more. From the lowest ranking soldier or family member, they were all treated the same in *her* hospital.

Holding the rank of Lieutenant Colonel in the Queen Alexandra Royal Army Nursing Corps, Ellis was brisk, business-like and to the point. Judging by her demeanour, Joyce suspected Ellis was accustomed to ruling the Cambridge with a rod of iron.

After a brief introduction, Ellis explained tartly that while a decision had been made to sign off Spencer's discharge papers, due to his injuries, he was still on a considerable amount pain relief. In *her* opinion, he wasn't ready to be discharged and should have remained hospitalised for at least another week. Ellis snorted her derision. Spencer, a difficult patient at the best of times, she added with feeling, didn't only test her patience, but had somehow managed to persuade the senior medical officer to discharge him against her advice.

Joyce smiled sympathetically and found herself mumbling an apology. Deep down, she felt almost vaguely sorry for the well-meaning, albeit austere, Ellis, who was probably unaccustomed to having her views countermanded by the duty senior medical officer. Ellis was a force in her own right.

Suspecting by now she probably had Joyce

on-side, Ellis sighed to draw breath. 'I suppose that I'd better show you the way.'

Joyce dutifully followed Matron down a long, seemingly endless wide corridor.

'Here it is,' Ellis announced, pausing outside a closed door. 'I'll leave you to it,' she said stiffly, with a slight inclination of her head.

Joyce thanked her again before opening the door.

Spencer was propped up on the bed, fully dressed. His eyes were closed, a pair of earphones clamped around his head as he listened to the radio. Joyce held back a little before closing the door. Spencer's face was still swollen and heavily bruised. A neat row of dark stitches snaked across his forehead into his hairline. Battered or not, he was lucky to be alive; they both were.

Joyce headed over to the bed, reached down and yanked the earphones plug out of the wall socket.

Spencer looked vaguely confused for a second before slipping the earphones around his neck and tiredly opened his eyes as Joyce perched herself on the end of the bed.

'I'm told *Matron* doesn't allow visitors to sit on patients' beds!' he grunted.

'Well, Matron's not, here is she? Besides, I have a feeling she'll be glad to see the back of you.'

'She certainly wouldn't be the first woman to say that.'

'God, I know how she feels.'

'I'm sure you do,' Spencer said, swinging his legs over the side of the bed and sitting up.

'How are you feeling?'

'Fine!' he lied.

'Matron thinks you'd be better off staying for another week.'

'The woman's a ruddy nightmare!'

'She's only doing her job.'

'Just get me home.'

'Are you packed?'

'Over there.' He nodded toward a small brown leather suitcase beside the wardrobe, his grip tightening as Joyce helped him off the bed. He tried straightening himself before murmuring an apology.

Joyce looked at him, askance. 'What's to be sorry about?'

'I'll try to make it up to you.'

She held his eyes for a fraction. 'Make up for what?'

He kept a tight hold of her hand to steady himself. 'I've been a bloody fool. You know that!'

Joyce brushed it off, jokingly., 'Tell me something new!'

'Jo, I'm being serious.'

'I'm sure you are.'

'Deep down, you must have known that I've always loved you.' Spencer smiled plaintively.

'I'm not a mind reader, no, I can't say as I did,' came her somewhat stilted response.

He paused a beat before adding, 'I've always

made it a policy never to get too close to officers I may end up sending to their deaths.'

'But you did once,' Joyce said softly.

It was obvious, she hadn't only hit a raw nerve, but he was still haunted by the loss of his fiancée, Sarah Davis, who'd died at the hands of a Nazi double agent during the war. Her loss had affected him deeply, and still continued to haunt him.

Even now, after all these years, in the dim gloom of night, an involuntary, subconscious wave of emotion occasionally swept over him. Where he'd once again, find himself engulfed in the black abyss of loss and guilt. Sarah, quite simply, remained the love of his life and still he blamed himself, for not only getting too close, but also for not being there for her, and that it had somehow influenced his decisions that led to her death.

Since that day, Spencer had always intimated he couldn't afford to let anyone else into his life. There'd been relationships, but none had ever lasted the course.

'So what's changed?' she whispered, gently tightening her grip around his hand.

'I need you,' he said, turning to face her.

'But that's just it. Nothing's changed, has it? I'm still in the firing line.' She smiled tearfully.

'You needn't be.'

'Spence, I can't give…'

'I'm not asking you to leave the Service.'

Joyce studied him warily, not quite sure what was

on offer. Her relationship with Garvan had already broken down because of his insistence she walk away from the Service. But it was in her blood, just as much as it ever was in Spencer's.

'Enid Burdis is due to retire in December.'

Joyce rolled her eyes. 'Are you joking?'

'No, do I look as if I am?'

'For Christ's sake, Enid's a bloody analyst, and a good one at that!'

'Come on; it'd be bread and butter stuff. You've done it before.'

'Yes, but that was back in the day. If you remember, I didn't exactly volunteer!'

'As good as Enid is, you'd bring far more to the table.'

'Maybe,' she said noncommittally.

'What's wrong?'

'I messed up.'

'I'm not sure what you mean?'

'Ivanov died on my watch.'

'One way, or another, Jo, he was always going to die on someone's watch. If not now, then it could have been ten, twenty years down the line. The KGB never forgives or forgets.'

'So, why bother?'

'Because the West needed him.'

'Was it really worth the cost?'

'Only time will tell, but Ivanov certainly thought it was worth defecting and placing his life on the line for us.'

'You're right,' she said, picking up his brown leather suitcase.

On the landing outside the ward, he looped his arm around her for support. 'How did it go with Cavendish?'

'Fine.'

'Just as long as there isn't any chance of a comeback on the Service, we can't afford to be seen...'

'To have blood on our hands?'

'Officially, we never have blood on our hands.'

She passed him a twisted smile.

'How did it go with the local police?'

'They seemed happy enough.'

'Good...I gather you bumped into Garvan at Cavendish's place.'

Joyce rolled her eyes. 'Well, let's just say, he wasn't quite so happy as the local plod!'

'Yes, so I understand,' he said drily. 'But whether Luke likes it, or not, he's one of us, and always will be!'

Reaching the bottom of the stairs, Spencer mumbled an apology of a sort and paused a second to catch his breath.

'I'd better get you a wheelchair from reception,' Joyce suggested brusquely.

'I'll make it to the bloody car park, even if it kills me!'

'At this rate, it probably will! You really are a stubborn old sod, aren't *you!*'

'Deep down, I guess that's why you love me…you wouldn't have me any other way.' He smiled.

'Don't ruddy count on it!' Joyce whispered, gently brushing her lips against his.

You've turned the last page.
But it doesn't have to end there.
If you're looking for more spy novels in the series, why not check out the website:
https://www.tobyoliverbooks.co.uk/

If you enjoyed, to Catch A Spy and Traitor, why not drop a review on Amazon and share your thoughts with other readers.

Keep Safe
Toby

Also available by Toby Oliver

Duty & Betrayal
The SS Brotherhood & The Nazi Connection

When a NASA scientist who worked for Hitler attends a conference in 1960s London, ex-Nazis and an international cast of spies materialize, hoping to steal secrets and settle old scores.

Book Viral

With accelerating plot twists that are more than just surprises delivered by rote, Oliver creates both suspense and an emotional impact with plenty of appealingly classic qualities that speak to his novel's theme. Rich in both resonance and elegiac melancholy he gives us marvellously nuanced characters without the frills and in doing so makes them feel organic and believable, never contrived. All brought vividly to life by Oliver with inventive narrative flair.

Literary Titan

This book reads exactly the way an old school spy movie would play out. No big flashes from explosions or high-tech gadgetry like we get from these stories now. Just operatives using their investigative and deductive logic skills to investigate, interrogate, and do what they can to capture the individuals they need. This is an exceptionally well-written book that is persistently entertaining and compelling.

The Downing Street Plot
An Agent's Revenge

Britain's Prime Minister has a target on his back— and the threat's coming from the inside. To save the PM in time, MI5 and the CIA must act fast.

Online Book Club
The author's superb writing is the primary appeal of this book. The craftily-worded scenes complement the political intrigue and subtle confrontation between the characters in the story, heightening the anticipation level in the book.

Advice Books
The author's superb writing is the primary appeal of this book. The craftily-worded scenes complement the political intrigue and subtle confrontation between the characters in the story, heightening the anticipation level in the book. For instance, I enjoyed the scenes featuring the tussle for control between Spencer Hall, and his immediate boss, the Home Secretary, Stanley Bradshaw. Furthermore, thanks to excellent historical references, such as the post war and the time followed after the rise and fall of the Nazism, the novel is highly recommended for readers in order they understand the important connections among the International intelligence services that, in theory, should defend us from terrorism.

Dead Man Walking
A Spy Amongst Us

The murder of a cabinet minister may be the break needed to unearth a suspected Soviet spy before the Allied victory of World War II turns into a bloodbath between comrades.

Online Book Club
The complex web of politics, manipulation, betrayal and the to top it all, the fact that no one is above suspicion, makes the book an exciting read. Readers who like political thrillers or spy novels based in the previous century should definitely give this one a try.

Historical Novel Society
London 1944 and the Normandy landings have not long taken place. False information is being fed to the Germans by double agents. A cabinet minister is found murdered and amongst his effects is an intended meeting with an unknown but suspected double agent working for Soviet Russia. Shortly afterwards a journalist and another MP are murdered, and attempt made on the life of the MPs secretary. Police Superintendent Luke Garvan, on secondment to MI5, is assigned to the case along with his boss, Major Spencer Hall and they attempt to uncover the identity of the spy. In a world of a

coalition government where MPs from opposite sides have to work together and where nobody can be trusted, we follow the pair as they untangle the webs of political espionage, old boys' clubs and double agents.

Also by Toby Oliver

Codename Nicolette

At the height of a bombing raid on war-torn London, a young woman is murdered. This was a swift, clinical killing with a single bullet wound to the forehead. The victim's connection to MI5 and Winston Churchill's secretive Double Cross Committee not only raises the stakes but rapidly spirals out of control, and becomes a race against time to track down the murderer before, it's too late, and the Allies counter-espionage battle against the German Intelligence is lost.

Mission Lisbon

When Winston Churchill's government learns of a Nazi plan to create a deadly new long-range missile, he orders British Intelligence to save a brilliant young French scientist, Jean Giscard, from the deadly clutches of a Gestapo assassin. Thousands of lives are at risk, from the weapons which affect the final outcome of the war against Nazi Germany.

Printed in Great Britain
by Amazon